A SOUTHERN B

SHEAR FEAR
AT THE
Curl Up and Dye

BELINDA PAGE

SHEAR FEAR AT THE CURL UP AND DYE

A SOUTHERN BELLE COZY MYSTERY

BELINDA PAGE

 Created with Vellum

CONTENTS

CHAPTER 1

"*T*his doo is too big, honey."

"It ain't big enough, shug."

Connie, the salon owner and stylist, was standing with a pair of scissors in one hand and a plate of chocolate pie in the other. She seemed more interested in the pie than her client's hair concerns. Trying to juggle the scissors and the pie plate, she failed miserably, and a piece of the delicious chocolate pie with its chocolate curls, chocolate curd and dark chocolate crust slowly slid off the plate, falling to the floor.

"Your hair will start looking like a wig if I make it any bigger, Paulette. And if I cut off any more, you'll need to wear one!"

Paulette, a regular client with a full figure, grumbled in her chair.

"Not that anyone would notice or care," snarked Claudette, the twin sister seated in the next chair with her hair wrapped in clusters of aluminum foil, her eyes glued to last month's issue of Pampered Gal, as she waited for her color processing timer to go off.

"Quit your fussin', and trust me, I'm the professional!" Connie barked, "You know I got you, Paulette!"

"Mhm," Paulette said with less confidence.

"Jenna, are you coming for this pie or not?!" Connie yelled to her salon assistant in an outer room. "I got no space to set it!"

HARPER HURRIED DOWN THE SIDEWALK, eager to get to her cozy haven, her favorite spot in all of Emerson. She was frantic about what had just happened, and if she didn't tell her gal pals, she felt like she would just burst!

Harper saw the usual group of regulars inside The Curl Up and Dye, chatting animatedly as Connie held a slice of chocolate pie. "Ooh! Is that chocolate pie I see?" Harper said to herself as she reached for the door handle.

The entire room shook as the salon door was flung open, causing the hanging bells to nearly fly off their hook. Connie dropped her scissors, but luckily didn't drop any of the pie. Paulette jumped out of her chair, Claudette accidentally tore out page 62 from the magazine featuring a handsome fireman in an ad, and Pearl, the manicurist, smeared hot pink nail polish all over her client's top knuckle."Oh, fudge!" Pearl was flustered.

A tall silhouette of a young woman in her early twenties stood dripping in the doorway, hyperventilating. Her dark blonde hair clung to her face, and her glasses fogged. She removed her oversized yellow cardigan, shook it out, and stomped the rainwater off her boots on the welcome mat. She closed the door gently and eyed the delectable treat. "Mmm, yummy pie!" she exclaimed.

"I do hope you plan to mop that up, Harper!" Connie yelled after Harper, who was disappearing into the back room. Picking up her scissors and composing herself, Connie began trimming Paulette again.

Harper hurriedly walked towards the back room without greeting the other girls or clients. She left a trail of murky footprints behind her. After some clattering, tinkering, and muttered cursing from the back, she emerged holding a fork instead of a mop.

Harper wordlessly grabbed the pie dish and began shoveling forkfuls of scrumptious chocolate heaven into her mouth with a vengeance, barely pausing between bites to swallow or breathe before scooping up more.

"You wanna leave some for the rest of us, shug? That thing cost me twelve dollars at Minnie's

Grocery," Connie raised her thin eyebrow questioning Harper.

Harper shoveled another dollop of chocolate cream into her mouth and gestured wildly with the utensil.

"They fired me!" She choked through mouthfuls of sugary decadence. Only it came out sounding more like "Dey fiwad muh!"

"Hey, dif iff goob, dib you make dif fwum scwatch?"

Oblivious to Connie's comment about purchasing the pie (and, for that matter, about mopping up her mess), Harper flopped down disgruntled into an empty styling chair and continued inhaling the pie. The others watched the pie almost disappear in horror, silence, and awe.

"You didn't bake that yourself, did you, Connie?" Paulette snarked in her usual instigating fashion, poking at Connie for it not being homemade.

Connie rolled her eyes and sighed with exasperation. "I have just about had it with all a' y'all! Harper Winslow put down the pie and clean up your mess. Jenna, get the rest of this pie in the dadgum fridge. Claudette, I saw you put that magazine page in your purse; put it back; that's property of the Curl Up. And Paulette, I will get you the recipe for the dadgum pie! It's effortless."

"As simple as going to the grocery store?" Paulette smirked between pursed lips and leaned back in her chair.

"Yes, Connie, I'm coming, I'm coming," Jena, a lithe brunette woman in her late thirties, rushed in from the arched doorway of the back room. "Here, if you don't mind, I'll take that, Miss Harper," she removed what remained of the dessert and disappeared again.

"Thank you, Jenna," shouted Connie, rinsing her scissors in a jar of Barbicide and wiping them on the waist of her apron.

"Oh, do be easy on her, Constance," Pearl said from her workstation. "Can't you see the poor child is distraught? Traumatized even? She ain' never been fired before."

"What's traumatized is my poor pie!" Connie piped up.

Sighing through her nose, mouth still full, Harper stopped and looked straight at Connie, eyes glazed, cheeks stuffed, wholly consumed by her now chocolate-covered sorrows of losing her *second real job*.

She swallowed, "If I don't have a job, I'll have to move back into my mother's house. Do you know what that *means*?"

"It means you'll never have a mortgage to fret over!" chimed in Claudette, and the two sisters laughed together in the same high-pitched warble.

"It means I won't be able to paint!" groaned Harper, kicking up one Doc Martens-clad foot onto the counter. She pivoted side to side in the chair. She knew Connie hated her rough riding in the chairs but couldn't resist the comfort of it since she felt defeated and wished for a large mug of steamy coffee to soothe her worries. Pie hadn't seemed to help.

The bells jingled above the door again.

"Mercy me, it is raining cats and frogs outside," a robust woman in a floral blouse and crocheted shawl carrying a large bundle cried out. A chorus of "Well, hey, girl!" and "How's it going, Miss Georgia?!" harmonized through the clouds of hairspray and nail polish fumes.

"Speak of the angel sent down from Heaven," Connie giggled and hurried over to wrap a towel around Georgia's shoulders; she guided her to the salon chair beside Harper. "Georgia, your wonderful daughter was just sayin' how much she adores you." Connie winked at Harper.

The elder Winslow laughed and kept still as Connie dabbed the rain from her shawl. Georgia tilted her head, smiled, and looked suspiciously toward her daughter. She was hiding her face with a massive grin, amused at Connie's attempt to schmooze her mother.

"What did she say about me now? Something about my gardening?"

Harper ignored the question and pointed to the bundle wiggling in Georgia's arms. Georgia unwrapped the wiggling throw blanket, revealing her beloved older beagle attached by a bright teal leash.

"Mama! What is Beauregard doing with you?"

Harper reached out and took Beauregard, "oh snookers, how ya doing, Beau? How's my Beau Beau?" She held him out before her. Beauregard was a hoot of a beagle, well-received by folks in town.

Local shop owners put out bowls of water and treats for him and other furry visitors, encouraging his escape-and-roam-the-town habit.

Harper made it her practice to inspect Beauregard for bumps and scrapes when she could get her hands on him. Satisfied with her inspection, Harper sat him down and gently patted his head. She looked to her mother, who shrugged her shoulders.

"He must have followed me somehow 'cause he showed up when I was at the butchers. Then he followed me here, the usual Beau' routine. Now, what have you been saying about my gardening?"

"Don't worry, Mama," laughed Harper, winking at her mom. "Nothing too harsh. But I do reserve the right to tease you about your gardening forever. I mean, after all, who could resist? Remember when you bought fifteen tomato plants, thinking they would grow into sunflowers? I swear Mama, it's too much."

Uproarious laughter filled the room, and Georgia rolled her eyes, grinning and accepting the ribbing.

"I may be a little green or maybe not green enough. There are worse things, my child!"

Harper waited until the chuckles died down before clearing her throat.

"Mama, I may as well tell you… I got fired… now, hang on before you say something; I know what you're thinking, but I wasn't late, and I wasn't napping, I was—"

"Painting. You were painting! Right, Harper? And on the clock, again! I just ran into your boss *at* the butcher's, honey. Why do you think I'm here? It was your job to *mix* the paint for customers, not use it for your creations." Georgia smirked at her daughter, who exhaled loudly and rolled her eyes.

"Customers, shmustomers!" Harper groaned and collapsed in complete dramatic form to the floor in defeat. "Sometimes I think this town is too small for me," and she sprawled across the black-and-white faux-Spanish marble. Muted snickers filled the room.

"Oh, Harper, get *off* the floor!" Jenna scoffed. Through tears of giggles, she gently nudged her with the broom. As Connie's assistant, she took on a professional tone, "Somebody might trip on you and sue poor Miss Connie for every penny she's got. Then all of us will be out of a job!"

"They can try and go after me," Connie chuckled. "There aren't many pennies here, and I'm still paying off this floor, which got installed five years ago!"

They all roared again with laughter while Harper pulled herself up with the help of Beauregard. She grinned and scratched his ears, and he was excited to have someone at his eye level for once.

"Harper!" Pearl spoke up just as the howls quieted down, "Why don't you work here, honey?"

"And do what?" Paulette teased, "Connie ain't in the 'portrait painting' business." Harper played along and stuck her tongue out at her.

Pearl sidestepped to Connie and draped an arm around the woman's broad, bare, freckled arms and shoulders. "She did go to beauty school, Con! Didn't you go to beauty school, Harper?"

"Well, yeah . . ." answered Harper with some hesitation. She glanced over to her mother while wiping her still-wet glasses with the sleeve of her cardigan.

"She dropped out," Georgia said in a matter-of-fact tone. They all looked from her to Harper. "Don't get my words out of sorts; she may have the finest eye for a color you ever saw, but, well, it was not her cup of tea."

Harper replaced her glasses and smiled. Her mom often had her back, especially when others questioned Harper's decision to leave beauty school in favor of a painting career. She knew her dreams were farfetched to folks from little old Emerson, South Carolina, so keeping her head high while working at the hardware store by day kept folks from openly sneering.

"Well, shug,' Connie sounded hopeful, "did you get good marks while you were there?" she tilted slightly and eyed Harper. She had known the girl since she was seven. Connie was protective of her crew and intensely discerning of anybody wishing to work in *her* shop under *her* name.

"I had some of the best grades in all of my classes, *especially* color theory," Harper replied, ". . . well, for the three semesters I *was* there." She sighed and relaxed her smile. "I just kept thinking I was meant for artistic painting."

Harper let the idea of a job at the salon swirl in her head. It may not have been the right time for her when she attended cosmetology school three years ago, but this was The Curl Up! She spent her teen years working here. She swept up hair and washed combs in Barbicide for extra cash during her summers, and now she spent most of her time there just because, well, because she could. She loved the place.

"Alright, Harper, we've been needin' a second colorist since Miss Bonita left; I'm worn thin even with Jenna's assistance. If you can cut straight, stay late, and come in on the weekend to get some extra training from yours truly, I might take a chance on you. But first, you'll have to show me them skills of yours, sugar. Got any courageous victims in need of a trim who might let you style them?"

The door's bells jingled once more, and the sharp clicking of heels against marble rounded the corner. Everyone faced the door like crane-necked owls to see *Miss* Melissa Montgomery waltz into the salon.

A knockout in Chanel tweed, she stood like a tall, svelte model beautifully tan from her summer in St. Tropez; dangling a pink Birkin handbag. She shook off and collapsed the matching pink umbrella.

"Laaadies!" she called out in a singsong voice fit for Broadway.

Harper rolled her eyes dramatically and watched as Melissa beamed and click-clacked away from the fluffy couches of the open waiting area and invaded the salon floor.

"So good to see all of you!" Melissa greeted the group. Harper was irked by her saccharine-sweet charade.

"Stunning highlights, Miss Montgomery!" Pearl looked Melissa's hair color over while organizing the large rack of polishes.

"Thank you, Pearl. Upon a girlfriend's insistence, I thought I'd try that new *Je Finesse* salon in Northville. Well, I hated it." She shrugged.

They all knew Melissa's routine—this well-to-do heiress of her father's French chocolate fortune—was a salon hopper. Melissa could do what she wanted with that kind of money, yet she always returned to Connie, of whom she thought the world.

"Get sick of the dog groomers, Mel?" Harper poked at her with folded arms.

"Hmph, don't call me 'Mel'." Melissa looked directly at Harper, who might have shrunk from her fiery glare. "You're probably *more* familiar with the groomer than me, Harper!"

"Whatever," Harper rolled her eyes and looked at Beauregard sitting at her feet. The beagle whined and nuzzled for more lovin' and resumed panting.

Both Harper and Melissa had grown up in the same town. They attended the same high school, the same after-school theatre programs, and the same . . . hair salon. They were like mixing water and oil.

Georgia had been taking Harper to Connie's salon since moving to Emerson. They scheduled once a month for Harper's trim and Georgia's blowout, eventually standing appointments twice weekly. Harper would sometimes help scrub and sweep in the salon after school. Melissa would also be there, sometimes interviewing the stylists for class projects and school newspaper articles.

Harper considered Melissa her rival.

Melissa did not consider Harper much at all.

Waving her hands excitedly, Melissa baby-stepped over to Connie, gave her a 'don't smudge my makeup' air hug, patted the older woman on the back, and pulled away with a big, dazzling grin.

"Did you want me to fix those highlights, shug?" asked Connie.

"Oh, no, Connie, I've come here to apply for a job!"

CHAPTER 2

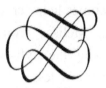

"*I*s this some sort of joke?!" Harper stood up, enraged.

"I beg your pardon?!" Melissa spun around on one heel and faced her accuser, equally enraged but with sophisticated restraint.

"You knew! You knew I'd be offered a job here, and you want to . . . sabotage me!"

"Now, why on God's green Earth would I ever be concerned with *you*?!"

"Because I have always been nothin' but a big punchline to you and your uppity friends! You want to keep the laughs comin'! You've always made it your personal goal to make my life miserable and break the awkward, nerdy girl's heart!"

"I gave you no mind in any of my plans," quipped Melissa.

"Why are you here, why now? Everybody knows you went to a fancy beauty school in New York! You boast your work all over social media! You've got, like, 60 thousand brainless followers! Why not apply at 'Jeet Fitness' or whatever it's called in Northville? Why the Curl Up?!" Harper was fit to be tied, spitting her words.

"Sit DOWN, Miss Winslow!" Connie was loud and firm but not hotheaded. "First, Harper, do not belittle my store. We may be a small boutique, but our draw is wide. Second, can you explain to me how Melissa was supposed to know about my job offer to you when I handed it out not thirty seconds before she entered?" Connie could not raise her eyebrows any higher.

"She was eavesdropping," Harper said in a dismissive tone.

"I WHAT?" Melissa retorted.

"Now, girls, you need to calm down right now," Harper's mother addressed them firmly. "There's not a dadgum thing anybody can hear through heavy rain outside, and you know it, Harper." She went on. "Miss Montgomery has every right to apply here. Maybe let her speak, and you'll learn something."

"To be honest," Melissa began, "I was offered a job at Family Hair Ties on Meadow Avenue— exquisite cucumber water, but so-so decor—I turned it down. Home is where the heart is. And *my* heart . . .," she placed one satin-gloved hand over her heart, her fingers gently grazing her pearl necklace, ". . .*my* heart… is right here at the Curl Up."

Paulette and Claudette 'awwed' in unison from under the bonnet dryers. Pearl and Jenna likewise swooned from their workstations. Harper's face dropped. She attempted to match Melissa's smugness, but it hurt her jaw. Georgia likewise glared.

"Now I don't know about no vegetables in water," Connie began, looking at Melissa. "But Harper here has already applied. I don't have the funds in the business to hire two of you. It does warm my heart to hear your sentiment, Melissa, so I want to offer you a fair chance. If you want in, the same rules apply to you. Find a client willin' to let you style 'em up, and I'll put y'all in a couple of salon chairs to watch your work. Whoever has the cleanest cut and neatest styling gets the gig."

Harper crossed her arms over her chest and caught the unwavering stare from her mother, whose face was saying, "Quit your pouting!" Unfolding her arms, Harper stepped forward.

"Sure, I'm down for a little healthy competition, Mel, if you are."

Melissa scrunched her face trying to hide her irritation about having to compete for a position she felt was rightfully hers.

"Didn't you get kicked out of beauty school, Harper?" she asked head cocked.

"I can cut it!" Harper squinted her eyes in frustration, then rolled them. "Pun intended!"

"We shall see," Melissa quipped, spinning on her heels.

"Not so fast," said Connie. She stopped Melissa in her tracks and picked through her selection of combs. "When an agreement occurs among proper ladies, we shake on it."

With that, Melissa extended her hand in a dainty manner, reached for Connie's fingers, and shook gently, with a delicate movement almost imperceivable. Next, Harper grabbed Connie's hand with gusto and shook it with enthusiasm. Then the two young ladies turned toward one another, embraced their palms, and shook with a quick, firm, single shake.

"We'll meet at the salon when doors open the day after tomorrow," Connie announced.

She looked back and forth between the two challengers for confirmation. "Arrive on time and with your volunteer client in tow. May the best stylist win! Do we have ourselves a 'trim-off?'"

"We have a trim-off," confirmed Harper.

"Sure," agreed Melissa.

Melissa smiled sweetly, head held high, and walked her kitten heels out the door. Her expensive perfume left a wake behind her.

Like a whirlwind, she had come and gone leaving everyone windblown. Georgia patted her hair to ensure her blowout was just right before breaking the silence in the salon.

"Well, well," she said carefully. "Guess we've got a little show to watch this week. Good luck, my love, not that I think you need it."

Harper smiled grimly. "I think I do need it. I feel a little in over my head, to be honest. Melissa is a hair and makeup influencer. Her work gets tons of likes and shares. Any chance of a healthy dash of nepotism, Connie?" she asked with a pouted lip.

"That's not how this works, my sweet," Connie corrected. "We ain't actually related."

"Yeah, but I'm your favorite, aren't I?" Harper whined.

Connie only smirked.

"Well then, I'll just have to earn it! How annoying!"

"Remind me, dear," Claudette raised to Connie, eager to loosen any lingering tension in the room. "How *did* you get your start in hairdressin'?"

"By accident!" chuckled the stylist. "As you may reckon, I was attending *law school* upstate."

"You?!" exclaimed Harper. "Studying law?!

"Oh yeah, shug. It was all very 'Legally Blonde' if you recall the film. It was the '70s; after all, women were moving towards empowerment, which was very much the big thing in those days. I wanted my piece of it!"

"Sounds boring," Harper said.

"It was God-awful boring," Connie replied, teasing Georgia's hair as it dried. "But, while at law school, I signed up for theater production on a whim: Joseph and the Technicolor Dreamcoat! I tried acting but couldn't quite make it. No, ladies, I found my real niche in the makeup and wardrobe side a' things. And it was all downhill from there. I quit law to study makeup, leading to hair and two thousand hours of beauty school. I couldn't cut acting, but ladies, I could cut hair! I apprenticed at an upscale hair salon in Richmond, South Carolina. I settled here two years later. The rest is, as you see, I like to say is 'Hair-story!" They all giggled.

"Remarkable," Harper stared into space and contemplated her life's path, wondering if strange twists might be waiting for her.

"Harper, dear, did you honestly get fired from Pullman Hardware for just a little paintin'?" Pearl asked from the cash register. "That Ben Pullman couldn't fire a gas stove!" she said with a cheesy grin.

With a sigh, Harper scrunched her face with embarrassment.

"No, not just a *little* paintin'. I used some cracked old drywall sheets for some paintings, figuring it might have been harmless. Luckily, I got just a warning for that."

The room stood still, anticipating further explanation.

"OK, so it was an unintentional incident. This vendor fella came in delivering a decent-sizedbox, and I assumed it was lampshades or something. Well, I opened the lid while holding it with one arm, and without looking, I stuck my free hand in and pulled out a stuffed rat!"

Jenna gasped. Pearl placed a shaking hand over her mouth, disgusted. "Stuffed?" she repeated through her fingers, brows raising.

"Taxidermized. A whole box full! And squirrels, too, which you know are just cute rats, and I—well, I didn't *mean* to do it, but I was surprised as all heck and sorta flung the entire box into the air and in the face of . . . Mrs. Flenderson."

"Mrs. Fannie Flenderson?" suggested Paulette.

"The one and only. Well, Mrs. Flenderson, she jumped back so surprised. . . right into a stepladder behind her. And that toppled over, along with Mr. Higgins, who was standing on it."

"Chester Higgins, the electrician?" interjected Claudette.

"Mr. Higgins, who was looking to purchase a large crystal chandelier, accidentally dropped it. The chandelier landed on a display of other fancy lighting fixtures, causing a domino effect of destruction. In the chaos, Mr. Higgins fell into the koi pond display, splashing water everywhere. Meanwhile, my now-former boss Ben was carrying a box of expensive LED lightbulbs and slipped on the wet floor. This caused him to accidentally throw the bulbs up and behind him. I attempted to leap in to catch them, but unfortunately, I wasn't able to reach far enough. Instead, I ended up pushing them into a display of glass shower doors, causing them to shatter." Harper finished her long explanation in one breath. She then paused and waited for the girls to respond.

The salon was very still. And very quiet.

Connie whistled long and slow, prompting another burst of laughter from the group. Harper smiled and allowed them to enjoy the moment. She looked down at Beauregard, sighed, patted his square head, and felt a twinge of sorrow.

"All in all," Harper added, "I caused only seven thousand dollars in damage, give or take a thousand!"

CHAPTER 3

*R*ain pattered softly against Harper's loft apartment's cold picture windows. Her cozy place was above and between Dough Re Mi—an artisan bakery cafe—and Green Acres, a flower boutique. Whenever stressed or depressed, Harper would step out onto the balcony and bask in the sweet and bold aroma of dark roast lattes and fresh-baked cinnamon muffins combined with pink peonies and red roses (and on Saturdays' flower shipments, a hint of lilac).

Her kitchen was all stainless steel with farmhouse-white cabinets flooded with natural sunlight. It was the least touched and, therefore, most organized room in the place, and upon entering the living room, one might think it was a different apartment entirely owned by another person. Equally flooded with light through open, sheer white curtains, it was a spacious room full of life and color. Beauregard's ceramic food bowls sat on the tile, each with pictures of bones and paw prints, which Harper had glazed and fired by hand.

Harper often lounged on her prized possession: A mustard yellow couch sat off to the side. Accompanying the sofa was her not-quite-matching bright yellow mid-century Formica coffee table covered in organized chaos:

- Artist's pens.
- Broken pieces of charcoal.
- Sketch pads.
- A stack of hairstyle magazines.
- An adjoining stack of art books.
- An array of essential oil bottles of varying emptiness.

A diffuser sat on one of the book stacks, emitting a pleasant, soothing lavender mist into the otherwise still air. A TV hung on one wall, playing a curated list of her favorite music to listen to while painting, surrounded by an array of plants from that shop below. The entire arrangement sat like a disorganized living room tossed to the side and forgotten about.

Harper was holding a to-go cup of vanilla cappuccino from the nearby coffee shop while standing in her living room. She was staring up at a partially painted canvas that was leaning against the bare brick wall. The painting was ten feet tall, which was a large piece for her, and she shifted from foot to foot while gently crimping the drop cloth below.

Harper sipped her coffee as Beauregard rested in the sunspot, absentmindedly licking away foam from her lip while contemplating her lack of work.

Splashes of blues and greens, as well as the faint outline of a figure, adorned the canvas. It was a piece she had struggled with for months. The more she stood and stared at it, the longer it took her to complete it. Her eyes began to blur from the constant attention she gave the painting. Fortunately, it was time for lunch, something she had been eagerly looking forward to.

It took her a few minutes to rinse her brushes in the color-stained plastic tub in her sink, silently promising to wash them as soon as she got home.

As she bid farewell to Beauregard, she gathered her long, brass-colored hair into a messy bun, creating an array of curls that sprang out in every direction. The loose tendrils kept interfering with her vision, and she had to blow them out of her face whenever she looked downwards.

Her mother would kindly tell her to rethink the look, while Connie might ask her who let her out of the house looking like 'that' and demand a re-do.

Harper's love for hairdressing and art didn't extend to herself, creating a contradiction.

On a day like today, she took the time to put on a summer dress and a pair of short kitten heels. Her dress was floral, flowy, and short enough to be flirty. Although she usually preferred a bohemian style, today she chose to embrace her southern roots and opt for a more gracious and classy look. She was heading for lunch at The Paisley Parlor, Emerson's first and only upscale tea house.

Tea was a weekly ritual for the mother-daughter pair. Harper eagerly anticipated the mid-afternoon tradition of sitting down with her mom over a piping hot porcelain pot of black tea. The two enjoyed an assortment of cucumber sandwiches, miniature cakes arranged in tiers, and flaky scones served with fresh strawberry jam and clotted cream.

The atmosphere was light and airy as if spritzed by the bergamot and peony perfume that hung in the room; as sunlight flooded through large picture windows and sheer champagne curtains, high tea guests flooded into the large dining room. With marble floors and painted gold arabesques on the ceiling, it was the prettiest, most picturesque place in a town painted only with the finest artist's brush. Always full of fresh flowers on each quiet table, so very inviting. Many young, modern debutantes sat around the white-clothed tables, sipping bubbly and herbal teas in their sundresses and pastel cardigans. Older ladies sat adorned in all their pearls and colorful dresses with matching coats and lavish hats as if dressed by Her Majesty the Queen herself.

Georgia Winslow's table had only two highly fashionable southern belles. They always had the same table, seated by the same window, which allowed in just enough sunlight to read the menus, yet not so much they had to squint at one another.

Harper arrived a few minutes late and noticed her mother in her usual spot, engaging in a conversation with the server, who was placing a pot of tea on the table. Harper made a beeline towards the table, trying to avoid hastily plopping down or slumping into her chair, as her mother might comment.

"Sorry, work ran late!" Harper quickly picked up her cloth napkin and flipped it over on her lap.

"I thought you got fired, where are you working?" Georgia asked incredulously as she fixed herself a cup of tea. She was often confused by her daughter but wasted no time getting her caffeine prepped. When annoyed, she could be a woman of few questions and comments.

"Painting *is* 'work' for me," Harper explained, pulling off her jacket and twisting it to hang on the back of her chair. "I was only late because I had paint under my nails."

"Typically, a product that goes on top, my love," teased Georgia. Harper gave a little smirk of camaraderie as they lifted their teacups—small, porcelain delicate things decorated with intricate hand-painted designs—and clinked them together, cheering the next day's event.

"Now," said Georgia, setting her teacup down. "There are three things you need to know about tomorrow's competition. Number one, know your opponent's strengths and weaknesses. Number two, know *your* strengths and weaknesses, and honey, number three, the rule to which you shall abide above all else—don't go lookin' for trouble."

Georgia watched her daughter's shoulders slump and her bright face go dim.

"Mama," said Harper, her anticipation having dissipated, "You got me all wound up just to tell me *not* to get into trouble?"

Georgia guffawed, tossing her head aside, allowing her silvery laugh to float in the air and fill the room. It echoed off the stucco, and some of the stuffier southern belles in genuine pearls bought for them by their wealthy husbands lent them some long-lasting side-eye.

Georgia paid them no attention. She was the type to buy her own pearls and was not bothered by their stiffness.

After Harper's parents divorced, her mother moved them to Emerson, South Carolina. Harper recalled her mother attending college courses in the mornings before secretarial work at the courthouse and then spending hours at night studying. Even though the divorce left her with enough money to allow a healthy start to a new life, Georgia Winslow was not one to rely on a man's income and was determined to earn for herself. She leaned across the table to pick up a tiny cucumber sandwich and admired every one of her lustrous pearls shimmering on her dainty neck.

Harper leaned in and selected a puff pastry, and before pushing the entire thing into her mouth, said, "She's trouble incarnate, ma."

She chewed, her cheeks packed like a chipmunk, and popped in another bite of a cucumber sandwich. Georgia was hard-pressed to stop her from speaking in such a state but tried.

"Yoo know, mom, dat waf—"

Harper stopped when her mother put her hand up and raised an eyebrow.

"Harper, dear, please! There are five senators' wives in this room."

It was Harper's turn to laugh, and she had to cover her mouth to keep from shooting a cucumber sandwich out of her nose. She and her mother sat at the table, maintaining their composure. However, they leaned towards each other and giggled for a moment before regaining their poise. Without acknowledging the catty stares of the local social society ladies, they poured themselves another cup of tea.

Soon enough, it was time for goodbye, and farewell niceties wrapped up their ritual tea. Harper kissed her mother on the cheek, and each went their separate ways.

Harper planned to stop at the salon before going home. She wanted to ask Connie if it would be all right for her to arrive early for the competition and organize herself. She would let herself in using the key Connie had kept under the backdoor mat for as long as Harper could remember.

As Harper entered the shop, she was taken aback to see Melissa wearing a pink apron that she had brought from home, custom embroidered with a glittery gold "M". Melissa's hair was perfectly curled as she was busy curling someone else's hair right in front of her. To Harper's surprise, Melissa was styling Connie's hair.

Harper considered Melissa, an "outsider." She stood at the entrance and didn't want to walk in feeling miffed and betrayed by Connie for allowing Melissa to style and trim her precious locks. Melissa spotted her and spoke up.

"Oh, *hey*, *girlie*," Melissa quipped up in that drippy saccharine voice, making Harper roll her eyes without restraint.

"Hey, shug!" Connie greeted her from behind a cooking magazine and a cloud of cotton candy-scented vapor. Harper eyed her as she snuck another hit from behind her magazine. Connie had quit smoking cigarettes some fifteen years ago at the behest of her late husband but began vaping when he passed earlier that year. Connie, in her grief, allowed herself some creature comfort compromise, at least when customers were not around.

Catching her eye, Connie waved her hand through the cloud of vapor.

"Oh, it's after hours, shug, ain't no clients in here unless you were lookin' for me to do somethin' with that mess on top of your head?"

Harper smirked, wiggling the loose bun on her head. It flopped back and forth. She caught Melissa with a half-smile and couldn't quite work out if it was sarcastic.

"No, thanks," Harper said. "I just wanted to ask if I can come in early tomorrow to set up, maybe practice a little on the mannequins. I can put the coffee on as well, and I know you like it real strong," she added upon seeing Melissa's face turn slightly sour.

Fully pouting now, Melissa kept separating pieces of Connie's hair, curling them with gentle hands, and Harper felt satisfied that she had staked her claim, at least for the time being. After getting the go-ahead from Connie, Harper left to go home.

Harper took little time to reach her block, even stopping for a frozen slush drink at the local Stop-n-Go convenience store on the corner. She was checking her phone for texts when she passed the front of the bakery holding her giant blue beverage, straw poking out of her mouth. She overlooked Gabriel, the baker until she walked right into him.

"Oh, Oops, I'm so sorry," said Harper, looking up and scrambling for an excuse for her oafishness. "I thought the bakery was closed."

"It is," said Gabriel with a light-hearted chuckle. He pulled a set of keys from his back pocket. "Just locking up now."

"Oh," Harper responded, nodding. They stood there for an awkward beat, Harper shifting on her feet and tugging at the strap on her large canvas bag, its contents inside clattering noisily.

"Um . . . the ovens are still warm and can fire back up in no time . . . did you want to pop in for something to eat?" It wasn't a privilege he offered liberally or to just anybody.

She wanted to say yes, he could see that she wanted to say yes, and the deep growl betraying her stomach's hunger wanted her to say yes. The slush drink had not filled her, nor had the meager cucumber sandwich from tea, but the way he smiled at her made her feel flushed and stammering.

"I'd better get some work done. Lots of . . . stuff to paint. Uhm, good day to you, sir."

And with that, she practically launched herself to her door and up her stairs, taking them two at a time. She could not believe how weird and awkward she had just behaved! 'Good day to you, sir?' Most of all, she had no idea why she lost the ability to act normally. Her hands trembled, struggling to insert her key into its lock. Were these . . . butterflies she felt?

DARK STORM CLOUDS drifted heavily over Emerson as Harper stepped out into drizzling rain the following day. The sun was beginning to rise but behind dark clouds. The air smelled fresh and clung to Harper's goosebumps. The droplets tickled and stung her face. Popping open a blue umbrella that looked black in the lingering dark, she walked the whole way without stepping in a single puddle until she reached the back door of the salon.

She lifted the mat, hmm, no key. Confused, she looked around, checking for another possible hiding place. Maybe Connie or Pearl had put it in another spot. She searched the potted snake plant, the wooden wind chimes above it, and the hide-a-key rock Connie used as a decoy, in her words, "to throw off burglars."

Harper hadn't noticed the slightly ajar door in her quest for the key, but realized someone had already unlocked it.

Harper pushed the door open, causing it to emit a low squeak. As she peeked inside, she heard a loud clap of thunder behind her, which made her scurry inside. She quickly shut the door, thinking that it had been blown open by the heavy winds of the storm.

She shivered, "Brrr!" and flipped on the lights.

She was in the break room. It was small but had everything they needed: A little round table with three chairs, an old olive-green refrigerator buzzing loudly (the "icebox" that Connie had for years), and the great Bunn coffee maker salvaged from a foreclosed diner. Harper started prepping to brew coffee immediately. As the beastly machine began sucking, steaming, and sprinkling the scalding water over fresh aromatic grounds, Harper smiled and thought about the trim-off.

She was excited but nervous about competing against Melissa. She wondered if Melissa ever felt nervous—or had any human emotions, for that matter—she walked into the salon and flipped on the lights.

Her thoughts were horrifically interrupted by the sight she saw before her. Smeared just about everywhere, across mirrors, and splattered on the floor was what looked like blood. It dripped down the back of a single salon chair. Embedded in the chair stuffing was one bloody pair of hair-cutting shears.

She blinked multiple times in disbelief, making sure that what she saw was actually real.

CHAPTER 4

*I*t took a moment to realize it must be blood.

This room looked like a murder scene. It looked like the blood had already started drying, and upon closer inspection, it could be nothing else. No hair dye in the world looked like this. It was streaked in places it shouldn't be - even on the walls and ceiling.

Harper horrified, backed out of the room ever so slowly, returning into the wobbly safety of the break room. Shaking, she pulled her phone from her purse and struggled to dial the police.

Emerson not being a particularly busy or crime-riddled town, everyone showed up in just five minutes.

Harper sat on the porch swing outside the salon, trembling while the wind rocked her slowly back and forth, one foot grounded. The weather had calmed down, at least enough to let the rain die. Numb from the chilly scene, Harper tugged her jacket tight, tucked her neck into the oversized hood and waited.

Harper felt a mix of relief and impending doom as two police officers arrived with flashing red and blue lights. She felt protected now yet overwhelmed by the implications of what had happened.

One officer began to get Harper's dazed, bewildered statement, and the other officer patrolled the salon, entering each closet and side room with her gun drawn.

"All clear!" the second officer shouted then came back outside, gun holstered, and took down some additional information. At one point, Harper heard her say to her partner, "There's a lot of blood in there, get Crime Scene, get Forensics, get . . . everyone." Hearing that made Harper's blood turn cold and she started shaking.

Before too long, "everyone" was there. Two detectives were pulling into the drive, both in the same car. Three more cars showed up full of police officers and crime scene investigators. Most ignored Harper completely and went about their specific tasks. Harper was kept there solely for the detectives questioning, who made a beeline for her when they arrived.

As they approached, Harper eyed them from beneath long, dark lashes. They looked familiar to her, and when they got closer, she realized they had been on the news some time ago for fumbling a twenty-year-old case of a stolen piece of abstract art. According to reporters, the cops had blamed it on being "far too" abstract.

One of them raised a hand, waving hello "Miss Harper Winslow, we need a word with you." His voice was steady, calm, and friendly enough.

"Detectives," Harper greeted them.

They looked from her to each other.

"You know we're detectives?" asked the taller, willowier one. "How?"

The man on her left, slightly shorter and muscular with a shaved head, raised his opposingly bushy brows in suspicion but kept his small mouth closed.

"Well, you're both wearing ridiculously long coats," Harper said flatly.

"Miss, my name is Detective Boychester, and this is my partner, Muffins." Detective Barnaby 'Barn' Boychester was a bully turned standup guy, now lead detective and local resident of Northville, the county seat and closest significantly sized town.

Harper knew his presence meant serious business. She was still shaking.

Harper bit the inside of her lip and squinted at them hypercritically, gaze lingering on Muffins. He smiled politely and nodded, quickly adding,

"Detective Henry Mufford, Miss, Muffins' just a nickname. I am a professional, I promise."

"Weren't back then," teased Detective Boychester under his breath, nudging his partner in the ribs.

The detectives chuckled together, and Harper could not help but feel slightly annoyed with how lightly they were handling the whole situation. She wanted to stand up and say something but restrained herself.

Harper recalled hearing about a small-time jewel heist wherein Detective Mufford (endearingly referred to as Muffins even by the press) had not only broken both legs but caught the thief in action. She recalled another time when Barn disarmed a bear holding a rifle. Harper found the story hard to believe until she saw the photo of Barn and the bear he'd wrestled in print. Rumor had it the bear was living his best life at the South Carolina State Zoo. These two guys were small-time heroes.

Harper looked right at them both, from one to the other, before clearing her throat.

"Well, what do you need from me?"

Detective Mufford raised his fist to his mouth, cleared his throat, and took hold of the belt around his waist, restraining his extra tire from popping out from behind his sports jacket. The detective reached into his pants pocket (not the one obstructed by his visible police-issue handgun) and pulled out a wrapped mini chocolate bar, which miraculously had not melted. He popped it into his mouth and chewed for a second before retrieving another. He held it out to Harper with a sympathetic smile.

"No, thank you," she replied.

Still in shock, Harper could tell he was just being nice, but the last thing she wanted or needed was a piece of chocolate. She needed answers. It seems they did, too.

Detective Boychester leaned against the porch railing, glancing up at the sky as the clouds began to part. The sun had risen, and birds sang in the trees around them, lifting some of the morning's gloom and replacing it with a romantic neighborhood surrounded by police.

"So, you told the 911 operator there was nobody there with you, correct?"

"Yes," answered Harper. She shifted uncomfortably in her seat on the porch swing.

"I walked in, saw a bunch of blood . . . everywhere, and I saw the scissors. So, I ran outside and made the call."

Barn looked at Muffins, ears perking up at the mention of the scissors.

"Now, where approximately did you see the potential murder weapon located?"

Eyes widening in panic, Harper almost stood up in alarm. "Excuse me, did you say murder weapon? Who was murdered? Is someone dead in there? You mean a potential murder weapon, right? What are you saying?"

Detective Boychester put his hands up haltingly, trying to calm her, "Now, now, calm down, Harper. Barn, here, he likes to get ahead of himself. Solve the crime a little too soon. Now, what exactly were you doin' here so early, shop doesn't open until ten o'clock?"

"And um, we know Connie likes to sleep in now and then, but, uh, we've been callin' to notify her, and . . ."

"No answer?" Harper added quickly. Her voice filled with worry. The expression on her face grew even more concerned.

"We've sent a patrol car to her house because she's not answering. She wasn't in her house either," explained Mufford, showing visible compassion for Harper, who sat there, still damp from the rain and cold. Shaking and looking miserable.

"Why don't we get you some hot tea?" asked Detective Mufford in an attempt to comfort her.

"We'll get hot tea once we finish," said Barn. He was looking down at her with suspicion. "You haven't told us why *you* were here so early."

Harper took a deep breath, scared by their questions and feeling her cold, stiff body start to hurt.

"I was opening the shop up early . . . we were supposed to have a friendly competition this morning. I wanted to prepare my station so I could beat this spoiled, thorn in my side, so-called friend. Connie originally offered me the job, and Melissa had to butt in, forcing a duel, but now, not only is the competition not happening, but something is going on here! And it's really bad. I mean, I don't want to think of any harm befallen Connie, but even if Connie is OK, what in the world happened in this salon?" Harper was out of breath.

"Miss Winslow, you're fixin' to pop a blood vessel in your head, there," Detective Boychester interrupted and pulled her out of her shocked, confusing moment of rambling. She was visibly distraught as he watched her silently and subtly wiping away a tear. His brow furrowed, and he glanced at his watch several times after thinking about what she'd just said.

"Exactly what time was this duel supposed to be?"

Before she could answer, cars pulled up and parked alongside the curb. Harper watched Pearl emerge from the driver's side of her mint green Volkswagen Beetle. Jenna came out of the passenger side, and behind them appeared an array of confused and troubled customers, community members, and well-wishers, all of whom crowded the scene and were greeted by yellow caution tape and officers and crime scene personnel asking questions.

"From the looks of the crowd pulling in, I guess the competition is 'sposed to be now," answered Detective Mufford, which got him an annoyed look from his partner.

The chaos continued, with people beginning to shout, cry, and flood the scene as police personnel struggled to maintain order.

"All a' the ones meant to be here for the competition; you see 'em? They all accounted for, Miss?" Detective Mufford asked, sticking a thumb back toward the group of ladies now all talking at once in worried tones to the unlucky police officer faced with corralling them.

She surveyed the scene, scanning left and right and then left again.

"No," replied Harper as her face wrinkled in anger. "Melissa Montgomery, my . . . would-be opponent, she's not here."

With unwavering tension, Boychester asked, "Harper, where do you suppose this Melissa Montgomery might be?"

Harper, eyes bloodshot and glassy from crying, slowly looked up at the detective. She was silent. She had no answer.

AFTER A FEW MORE QUESTIONS AND a hot cup of tea, the detectives allowed Harper to leave. They spoke with the salon employees, whom Harper had kindly pointed out, giving them each a "good luck" nod on her way to her mother's car.

Georgia had arrived in heels, brightly colored curlers, a diamond bracelet from her ex-husband, and a terrycloth robe. After informing a confused Harper that she had made a panic-stricken dash to get dressed and save her only child in a "fit of fright, only a mother could understand," they drove home to Georgia's estate.

After winning the divorce settlement, she decorated the place in her own unique and glamorous style. She had decorated the beautiful oak circular staircase with a pink and red feather boa left over from the most recent Valentine's Day. The living area was bright and sunny, full of books, and three olive green cabriole sofas surrounded a lit wood-burning fireplace.

Harper sat on the rug before the fire, dressed in her mother's pajamas and an uncomfortable showy camisole, which she covered by wrapping a large wool blanket around herself. Beauregard laid on her lap the entire ride to her mother's, and now he snored breezily in front of the fireplace beside her, kicking his leg every so often when she'd rub his belly. She

43

warmed in front of the fireplace, saying nothing and petting Beauregard, whom she had insisted on picking up from her apartment before going to the comfort and safety of the Winslow house.

Georgia had invited the rest of the crew from the salon over, and they showed up one by one, each complaining of the wind, the cold, their trauma, and the police officers.

"Incompetence!" said Pearl, huffing as she hurried over to sit on a sofa nearest Harper. She put her hands out to soak up the warmth of the flames.

Pearl rolled her eyes, tossing off her ivory pea coat and saying, "Could you believe those detectives and their questions? They asked me the same thing seven times!"

Georgia rolled in a small silver coffee cart displaying tea, coffee, cream, and sugar. She passed around a couple of trays of shortbread, and as everyone settled in, they began the serious discussions.

"Do you think she's dead?" Jenna asked softly, putting their obvious concern out there. She had arrived looking windblown, recounting how she had run into the twins, Paulette and Claudette, right after police questioned her. They were utterly panicked.

Pearl scoffed indignantly while Georgia's eyebrows shot up. "No, Jen, of course not; she's just fine. I'm sure she'll turn up." She gave her friend a little slap on the shoulder with one of her gloves, which she removed one at a time before stretching her elegant long fingers apart to air them out, her painted nails as perfect as ever.

"And just where is Melissa?" asked Harper, looking upset and frustrated. "She's the only one besides Connie who didn't show up, so where is she?"

"We've called her, hon, but she's not picking up," said Georgia, perched on the arm of a sofa.

"We'll find her, *and* we'll find Connie," said Pearl quite determined. "Now how can us girls help?"

They spent the remainder of their time together discussing who would look after the salon and when they could get back in. Detective Mufford had told them it would take a day or so until the crime scene would be cleaned up. Harper struggled to think how cleaning it up would or could help erase the memory—at least in her mind—of the bloody salon. She was desperately hoping Connie would appear any minute now laughing and telling them there's 'no use in crying over spilled hair dye' or some other light-hearted explanation for a pair of shears embedded in her salon chair.

'Right, who am I fooling,' thought Harper.

Still hoping Connie would appear soon, Harper's mother dropped her and Beauregard outside her

45

apartment. Georgia waited and watched, ensuring her daughter and Beau' made it safely inside before driving off. Exhausted, Harper trudged her way upstairs, letting Beauregard inside, and grabbed her clear plastic bucket full of paintbrushes, which she brought down to rinse at the hose spigot out back.

Washing her brushes was therapeutic and calming. It was as much of an escape as painting. Waves of nostalgia washed over her whenever she smelled her oil paints and turpentine or heard classical music, as it was always reminiscent of her time spent in art classes.

As she lowered the bucket of brushes into the exterior trough, she heard a noise. Looking over, she noticed Gabriel exit the bakery and load a box of muffins into the delivery van.

"Hey," she greeted him and cleared her throat, not realizing how weak she sounded. She must have looked even worse because when Gabriel turned around to greet her, he reeled back slightly, brow-raising and teeth gritting.

"Oof," he said. What happened to you?" he asked.

Harper sighed and said with exhaustion, "I don't even know where to begin, it'll be all over the news soon."

Upon hearing this, Gabriel's eyebrows raised as he watched Harper look longingly at the freshly baked muffins in the wheeled bakery case.

"I'm surprised you didn't collide with me this time," Gabriel teased, encouraging Harper to tell him more. He smiled, catching Harper's eye, who faintly smiled back.

"I'm exhausted physically, but I'm still pretty sharp," she admitted.

Taking the opportunity, he offered one of his delicious baked goods. "You look like you could use a cinnamon muffin. The last batch just came out of the oven and they are still warm."

His offer was tempting because although there had been countless trays of finger sandwiches and shortbread cookies passed around at her mother's house, Harper had been just too cold and in shock to eat.

Now, the mere smell of warm cinnamon made her stomach growl. Gabriel heard it and chuckled. He picked the biggest muffin with sour cream icing oozing from its cracks on top. He handed it to Harper, who delicately removed the foil muffin liner.

"This isn't a muffin! It's a cupcake full of deliciousness," Harper could feel the heavy weight of the thick pastry lifting it to her mouth.

Gabriel laughed, watching. The baked goodie covered her entire face when she held it up. She dove into the comforting goodness, her mouth ever so full, steam rising from the muffin where she'd taken her bite. It was intoxicating, and Harper felt particularly grateful after her long full day. Thank you," she said. This muffin is incredible. I'm almost embarrassed to say I've lived up above this bakery for six months now, and I've never once tried anything."

"Oh, I know," Gabriel replied, smiling at her. Harper returned a puzzled smile.

"How do you know that?"

"I'm the head baker!" he laughed. "I am here all the time, and besides, I've noticed you coming in and out, always in a hurry, always wearing your jeans all covered in paint. I would know if you stopped for a nibble."

His last comment made Harper blush and tuck her head down into her shoulders a bit.

He went on. "You don't seem to notice much of the bakery activity with those earbuds you wear, but whew," he waved his hand in front of his nose, "I notice you with that stuff you use . . . it's pungent!"

"Oh, yes, my turpentine, it's smelly," she said.

Gabriel smirked. "Don't you do anything else but paint?"

A bold question coming from someone always at work, Harper thought.

"Well, I was supposed to cut someone's hair today. I was trying to get a job at the salon, but . . . well, you'll learn soon enough what's going on, news travels fast around here."

Gabriel chuckled at the remark and nodded, knowing he had only moved to Emerson a year ago. Still, even he had learned that gossip around town was hot, readily available, and dispensed more willingly than a two-year-old learning to share his Cheerios.

"Oh, so the salon is where you go all the time. You're a hairdresser, too?"

Harper shrugged, and although Gabriel was a comfort to her, she was still in a funk. She could not stop seeing the horrific scene in her mind. She tried to continue with the conversation. "Well, I think I'd be good at it and I need a job. I want to work there. I used to go to a hair academy upstate, but I . . . but, well, let's just say I need some practice," she finished, deciding at the last minute not to let him know she had dropped out.

Gabriel twisted his mouth in thought and began running his hands through his hair. Thankfully he had wiped them off first, but Harper still saw some flour on his dark brunette strands.

"I, uhh . . . I could use a trim . . . how about practicing on me?"

Looking and smiling at Harper, she felt those butterflies again. She glanced from her drying brushes and back to Gabriel who said, "My hair grows fast, and I hate shoving it all under a hairnet."

She looked his locks over and wanted to do something to avoid talking about her morning. "Your hair *is* a little bit shaggy, sure, why not? Let's give you a cut. First, I've got to feed Beauregard; so, come on up."

"Who?" Gabriel asked as he followed Harper. She laughed her way up the stairs.

$\mathcal{H}$arper and Gabriel spent the evening making drinks and playing with Beauregard before the main hair-cutting event. Harper sat the baker down on a tall stool at the kitchen island and ran to retrieve a pair of shears she kept in the bathroom junk drawer.

When he saw scissors, Gabriel felt anxious. Nervously gripping his wine glass, he looked down to Beau for encouragement. He was curled up at his feet with his square hound head tilted curiously toward Harper, who was approaching with, frankly, a devilish grin on her face.

"You look way too excited with those shears!" Gabriel gulped.

"That should make you rest easy!" Harper protested, walking around the chair to stand behind him, and continued, "I'm excited to hone my craft, to practice, oh, ...wait, I'm forgetting something."

Skipping to the bathroom, she reemerged with a large salon apron she'd swiped from Connie's. Then she walked back over to Gabriel, sitting still in the chair. She draped the apron over him and clasped it at the back, leaving enough room for him to breathe.

"Man, you got this down; you must spend a lot of time in there." Gabriel eyeballed the apron monogrammed with many bedazzled 'C's.

"It's my happy place, like a second home," explained Harper. She tried not to think about the possible threat to her happy, safe place and changed the subject to baking. "So, you must spend all your time downstairs with the ovens. I mean, even now, you smell like freshly baked bread."

Gabriel wasn't surprised to hear this. They laughed as Harper picked up a spray bottle full of water and aimed it at the back of his head.

"Sit still now," she giggled and announced, "This will only hurt a little."

THE NEXT DAY, Harper woke to the sounds of Beauregard dragging his empty food bowl across the floor. She fed him and hustled to get ready to meet the girls at their beloved teahouse. She was eager to go, mainly for the comfort of friends and partially for the cucumber sandwiches.

She walked into the Paisley Parlor, and there they were, sitting around the usual table. She descended into her chair amidst the chattering of celebrity gossip and the talk of trends from the latest style magazine. It usually amused her, but now it was calming her. As soon as Harper arrived, she felt comforted by the familiar faces gathered there. She was eager to dive into the obvious subject of the crime and compare notes with the girls. Had they heard from Connie? Heard of any updates to the investigation?

They greeted her with muted excitement, and Harper scooted her chair closer to the table. Everything seemed muted and toned down without Connie. Her absence removed some color from the room.

Never one for gloom and doom, it was Pearl who reached over and gave her a quick hug. "We've gotten so many floral bouquets from people' 'round town at the shop. It's gonna be overflowing with flowers when we reopen! Have you been by?"

"No, I figured I should steer clear."

"But, hon, everyone's been goin' by to lay flowers on the porch. Everyone in town. You really ought to swing by and see, it'll warm your heart how folks show their love for Connie."

"She's not dead, Pearl, for goodness' sake," Georgia interjected between sips of tea. "The woman's only been missing a few days."

Pearl busied herself from the tense conversation by pouring another cup of tea and picking a ripe plum from the fruit bowl.

Jenna ran a nervous finger through her dark, springy curls, "Well, um, Harper, sweetie, . . . I saw Melissa! She was walking into the fancy organic grocery market, the one right by the corner where the police station is, and boy, she looked distraught."

Everyone's eyebrows shot up, and all faces flung around to look at Jenna.

"Wait! You saw her? Do you think the police must have questioned her at the station?"

Pearl scoffed, leaning forward, and rolled her eyes dramatically, "she probably had to go pick up a whole case of fancy organic water. Rehydrate all the tears she probably spilled for the police." In a calm voice, Pearl said, "I heard little ol' Melissa Montgomery never actually finished beauty school up there in New York."

The table collectively gasped. Servers and patrons nearby gave them the side-eye, but the girls always paid them no mind. They all fully locked on to Pearl, who continued, "I heard from my cousin, whose daughter went to school with her, that she had a panic attack in the middle of a practice session and ended up chopping some poor girl's hair off, like, five inches!"

"No!"

"Yes!"

"Did they sue? I would have sued."

"Wait, wait, so she flunked out and left?"

"Well," Pearl went on after the table had regained composure, "Apparently, she flunked out after her hair-chopping incident and moved home. Probably why she's so desperate for the same position, Harper!"

Harper sat up, surprised, "I don't think she is desperatefor *anything*. Her family has plenty of money, she could never work a day, and she'd be fine."

"But you can't put a price on feelin' useful, hon," offered Georgia.

The sentiment was one to remember, but Harper could not shake her disdain for Melissa. She had shown up for years smelling like a rose and never seemed to tell the exact truth twice. Harper was beginning to wonder, just where *was* MissMelissa?

At that moment, a familiar-looking woman, tall and lithe in stature, walked up. Her long legs met the hem of a purple shift dress covered by her long, voluminous red hair. Sunlight from the window bounced off her shiny locks, creating a dreamy, bright yellow halo around her frame. She smiled a Hollywood white grin and looked right at Harper.

"Oh, my, gosh. Are you kidding me, Harper Winslow? I haven't seen you since high school!"

Her voice was familiar, deeply rooted in the south, her accent only enhancing her enthusiasm about everything, and suddenly it clicked for Harper, who gasped, "Charlotte, yes, now I remember! I admired how you just left high school, moved to Paris, and pursued your graffiti-style canvas art. You were so brave!"

Some confused and curious glances passed around the table as quickly as the cucumber sandwiches, not unnoticed by Harper. She ignored them, intrigued by Charlotte's risky habits. Truth be told, Harper would have loved to drop out of high school, run away to Paris, and pursue her artistic passion. Especially since Harper was finding a career as an artist so difficult to achieve, Paris may have given her a leg up!

"How is Paris?" Harper was smiling at Charlotte and enjoying her pleasant social surprise. True, seeing Connie would have been a welcome sight, but it was a breath of fresh air to see Charlotte, a friendly face she'd missed for a while.

Charlotte smiled, turning her palms up to the sky, and shrugged, "I wouldn't know, as you can see," she said with a halfhearted smile. My Paris exhibit closed, so I'm moving on. The good news is, I am opening a gallery here, in Emerson. What about you, Harper?

56

Tell me about you. Have you stopped painting? And if not, do you still have your abstract style?"

"I just could never stop painting or my abstract style!" Harper said with a wink, "You know I love using color too much. Honestly, my struggle is finding a place to showcase my pieces. I can't find a good spot anywhere."

Tossing a hand up to her delicate handcrafted necklace, Charlotte gasped with delight. "Well, then, this is great news! The gallery I'm opening up could use another artist in the mix. I had planned to partner with another artist by offering a small space or boutique to show their work. We would have a soft grand opening in a few days, then our first big gallery-wide event next month. The space I'd rent to you could handle say, ten paintings, and three full walls, at your creative discretion, of course. Are you interested? Would you want the opportunity for the boutique space? And do you think you could show your work at the opening? I'm quite serious, Harper; I'd love to have you as a junior partner!"

It took a moment for Harper to pick her jaw back up off the table, where she was sure it had fallen into her empty saucer. She looked over to her mother, who grinned and nodded excitedly, trying her hardest to remain quiet and not squeal. The rest of the ladies followed suit.

Harper could hardly believe what she heard, an opportunity to have her own space in a trendy new gallery. She has dreamed of this for so long, so, so, long. But, oh, dear, with everything going on, she isn't ready financially. No job, bills on the steady, and no salon gig now. Unless...

Harper quickly refocused back on the table and was more than ever determined to make this offer work.

She needed the salon job now more than ever. She must do something: help find Connie, get back to winning the styling competition, get some income rolling in, and pull her life's dream together!

Suddenly, a wave of guilt washed over Harper. She felt guilt for feeling happy, shame for entertaining the idea of doing an art exhibition, and guilt for considering a partnership when so much was happening. She felt entirely selfish.

It broke her heart to not have Connie here. She would have been the most enthusiastic supporter of this opportunity and most encouraging of a career in art.

Turning back to Charlotte, Harper said reluctantly, "Well, of course, I'm more than interested and very grateful for your offer. But, I . . . I'm wondering if it's the best time for me to take you up on it. I don't know if you have heard, but my friend,

Connie, is missing, and we're still not sure of how serious it is."

"Oh, honey, I did hear! I didn't know Connie was your friend," Charlotte gave Harper a sympathetic look.

The table spoke up. Georgia was first after dabbing a spot of jam from the corner of her mauve lipsticked mouth. "Now, Harper, darlin', you sure you want to pass up an opportunity like this?"

"Of course, she shouldn't give it up!" cried Pearl, usually the quiet, soft-spoken of the bunch. She surprised herself with her outburst, but Jenna backed her up.

"Your mama's right, babe. You shouldn't pass it up!"

Pearl nodded in agreement, her loose curls bouncing against her shoulders, and added, "You've got nothing to feel bad about, girl. Connie knows how much you love her and how much you would want her to be safe. You're following the dream you've shared with her for so long; it's what Connie would want for you."

Harper agreed; this was very true. Connie had always supported her art endeavors, even allowing Harper to sit for hours in her shop. She drew portraits of clients who came in for their appointments and documented everything in her sketchbook. By the time she entered high school, Harper had several sketchbooks full of portraits of women with beautiful hair.

From the buzz of excitement around her, she could also tell that everyone wanted her to accept. Her head spun, concentrating hard and trying to organize her thoughts quickly. Could she help find Connie? Would it be in time for the gallery show? What if the police can't figure it out? How could she do any better? Calming herself and slowing her thoughts, she sorted out the many details of what must come together.

Harper figured she would have to help find Connie, she would have to do it quickly, and she would have to get that stylist job to launch this opportunity with her own funds and talent. Harper feared failure right now. Especially with the not-so-stellar results of her past attempts, failure to launch could potentially be the 'icing on the cake" of her social ruin.

"OK," Harper said, "I'll do it!" Classic Harper.

Charlotte and the whole table burst out in relieved, excited, overjoyed smiles and applause.

Grinning, Charlotte squealed and leaned down to hug Harper around the neck, whose eyes bulged at the intrusion.

Fighting to breathe, she gently patted Charlotte on the back and managed a laugh. "OK, OK, she squeaked out before Charlotte pulled away, still grinning.

"Tell you what, Harper, why don't you come to the gallery for our soft grand opening and take a tour? We're featuring some great artists in the main space, so you could meet other artists and mingle, get a feel for the place, and see what it will be like for your big event!"

Charlotte's offer was too generous to pass up. "Sure, I'd love to!"

"Great, I'll send you the details!" Charlotte squealed before blowing her a kiss, waving goodbye to the rest of the table, and hurrying off. "Gotta skedaddle. I'm meeting up with the curator to review the opening plans. Wish me luck!"

As they watched Charlotte flounce away toward the doors, it only took about ten steps before the table erupted.

"She's so tall and glamorous!" gushed Pearl. "I always *knew* you'd find a place to show off that talent, girl!"

"Connie would be proud of you, honey," Georgia said, pouring her daughter a warm cup of tea.

Harper felt her nerves and her stomach tighten up in a knot. What have I gone and done now, she thought? Am I setting myself up for yet another 'Harper failure?" Shaking off her doom and gloom, she sat upright and thought, no time to waste.

HARPER WRAPPED it up at the soiree with her gal pals and left. As she was leaving, she couldn't resist grabbing a to-go cup of tea and a baggie of glazed scones to enjoy on her way back home.

She was in deep thought. Her mind was boggled with the notion of Connie gone missing. She couldn't shake off the grim scene of the salon flashing through her mind. The puzzle pieces of how, when, and why just wouldn't leave her alone. She couldn't resist her curiosity and sense of urgency. She had to explore further. She impulsively made her way to Main Street toward the salon.

Harper wondered what she would find. She just wanted to stop by and check it out from a safe distance. It was dark outside. She saw the yellow caution tape but couldn't resist crossing under it to stroll around to the back. She fumbled around the door area looking for the key. She remembered the crime scene cleanup crew had ultimately found the key and said it had been sitting in the dirt flowerpot next to the back door. She felt around on top of the flowerpot and found it. Just a quick look, she told herself, what could it hurt?

She had not planned on using that key to unlock the back door and go inside. She had certainly never intended, she told herself, to go snooping through the shop. Yet here she was.

Walking through the dark space, she held up her phone light, illuminating various nooks and areas around her. The place was practically empty since the police and cleaning crew had cleaned out jars full of combs, bottles upon bottles of shampoos, conditioners, and serums. Everything had been gathered, cleaned up, and tidied; the blood was no longer there. Once covered in dripping bright red blood, the salon chair looked entirely normal, betrayed only by the deep gash across the top, where the pair of hair-cutting shears were found deeply embedded. No longer there, Harper assumed the shears had been bagged and taken for evidence, as most of the things spattered in blood had been.

Harper was driving herself batty with questions she couldn't possibly answer, but her persistence endured, and she ventured further into the main room of the salon. She stared at the empty chair, seeing the image in her mind, the bloody shears stuck in the spot where the stuffing was coming out.

Someone was a crazed killer. There could be no other conclusion. They must have aimed for Connie and got the chair instead.

She passed an empty row of shelves that usually held Connie's favorite color-correcting shampoos. She was about to shine her phone flashlight on a nearby counter when she heard a clatter. She turned quickly to investigate.

Her phone lit up the silhouette of someone running   toward   her.

CHAPTER 6

*A*ll Harper could see in the scant light was a blur of a scarf, an oversized coat, a wide-brimmed floppy hat, and a dark figure lunging toward her; she was knocked off her feet and smacked on the tile floor. Her phone flung out of her hand, clattering a few feet away under the counter, lighting up the underside, not much light, but enough for her to see a bit better. She could think of nothing but to get to her phone and scrambled to her feet. Bending down, she instinctively grabbed it and whipped it around to shine the light toward the figure. She saw no face, but a figure bundled in clothes.

Incredibly expensive-looking clothes.

"You've got to be kidding me; you are not..." Harper scrambled for the masked person, who let out a little yelp and tried to run for the foyer entrance. Harper grabbed the escaping intruder by the scarf and yanked away the garment to reveal none other than Melissa!

"What?!" Harper could hardly believe her eyes now burning with anger. "Seriously?!" she shouted. "What are you doing here? Are you mad? I cannot believe you, Melissa! Actually, I can believe it, of course! I suppose you are looking for someone else to kill?"

Melissa was the one who looked shocked now! Gawking back at Harper, Melissa harshly tugged her scarf out of her hands. "Excuse me! Don't be ridiculous! How dare you! I should be the one to ask, what are *you* doing here, and why would you say such a horrible thing ?!"

Harper scoffed, stepping back, and folding her arms across her chest. "Don't play stupid, Melissa. You were the only one who didn't show up the other day. You were to be here for our styling duel. Where were you? And where have you been? What could keep you from helping, getting in touch with any of us, or caring about Connie, the person you say you care so much about? Hmm? "

Melissa stood wide-eyed.

Harper continued passionately. "We have all been overwhelmed with concern about Connie, so very worried about her, no one has even thought to ask where 'Miss Melissa Montgomery' might be! So, now

I'm asking! You were supposed to be here, and yet, not a peep from you regarding your whereabouts, your last-minute 'no show' to the competition. Do tell, Melissa, this ought to be good."

Melissa broke down in sobs, big tears welling up in her eyes, and her supposed smudge-proof mascara was smudging while she ugly-cried.

"Oh, come on now, stop it... stop... stop!" Harper grabbed Melissa's hands from hiding her tear-stained face and placed them to her sides. She pulled Melissa into a quick, awkward, reluctant hug.

Harper was surprised at herself and, for once, actually felt sorry for her.

"Settle down now. Get a grip. *Please* tell me what in the world is going on!?"

Melissa, still sobbing, shuffled over to the wall, and felt for the nearest light switch. She flipped it. The two girls blinked at the sudden change in exposure, and Harper confronted Melissa again.

"Why are you here, slinking around in the dark, Melissa? And crying? In patent leather heels."

Melissa dramatically flopped down into a salon chair—the same one with the giant scissor slash through it—and promptly jumped back up and cried even harder. "I'm looking for *my scissors*, OK?!"

Harper stared back, shocked. "The scissors were yours?" she whispered. The idea that Melissa might be capable of such an atrocity was more than she could imagine, but just the same, she slowly backed up. "What did you *do*, Melissa?"

Melissa sobbed harder, flopped back into the chair, and shook her head, putting her hands up defensively. "I didn't do anything! That's the whole point! I think someone is framing me!"

Harper could barely understand her through her tears and snot. She quickly realized that this puddled Melissa mess wasn't an immediate threat. Dropping her shoulders and rolling her eyes, Harper marched forward and spun Melissa around in the chair. "Talk to me," she demanded and rummaged through a nearby drawer, retrieving a makeup wipe. She handed it to Melissa, who sniffled and wiped her face before explaining.

"Those scissors have *my initials* on them," she said while breathing in quick little gasps to help hold back her sobs. "They're from an entire professional set, which I lost a few weeks ago. I got scared when I heard something awful may have happened here, and . . . well, I was unsure if the police in their scene investigating may have found them by some chance, so I snuck in here to try and find them myself. It would have looked so very bad if my scissors were involved! I swear, Harper, I would never hurt anyone, especially not Miss Connie!"

Harper studied her now. Through all this bravado, dramatic sobbing, and tears, Melissa's once-perfect hair, now tangled and ruffled, was all Harper needed to see to know she was earnest. Still, she had more questions.

"Why didn't you come to the trim-off?"

Melissa shifted and sighed, seeming uncomfortable, "I don't see how that's important."

Harper folded her arms across her chest again and gave her a look.

"Oh? I show up to the salon first thing in the morning and find it looking like a one-shade Pollock painting, and you don't think it's important?! You're annoying at all hours, aren't you?"

"Fine, Harper, I just . . . I couldn't. I couldn't compete with you!"

What an admission! Harper was surprised at what she was hearing and let her continue.

"I was intimidated, OK? I've seen what you can do. You're always practicing on your hair, your mom's hair, and the mannequin's hair. I can barely get Miss Connie to let me practice on her, and it's not like I have a mom, and now I don't even have Conn—"

Melissa stopped abruptly, realizing what she had just blurted out. Her cheeks turned a shade of rosy pink, revealing her embarrassment at expressing feelings toward Connie. She looked down at her feet.

Harper did, too, letting Melissa's vulnerable expression sink in. So that was it, Melissa viewed Connie as a mother figure. It was easy to understand. Harper recalled their preteen years when Melissa's mother had often disappointed her. She never attended ballet recitals, parent-teacher conferences, town festivals, or goings-on. Meanwhile, Harper and Georgia talked excitedly about the upcoming Emerson Harvest Fest, the Emerson Jingle Bell Parade, and Emerson's Spring Fling Flower Fair, all of which they were heavily involved in making crafts or baking goodies for the events. She was fortunate and only now understood Melissa a little bit more.

Harper thought back on Melissa and how she would walk around the festivities with 'the girls.' They were a small gaggle of upper-class debutantes who, in high school, followed Melissa around like puppies. Come to think of it; Harper *did* always see Melissa stop to spend time with Connie, laughing over a sample of local apple pie or even riding a few rickety carnival rides together during the big yearly fair.

With a sigh, Harper glanced around the room. She was seeing a side to Melissa she never knew. "I'll help you look," she offered.

While they looked in every nook and corner for the hair shears, Harper thought how ridiculous this was—searching a crime scene probably already scoured over for a pair of scissors! Considering the news media had reported the shears as the potential "vicious, bloody murder weapon," it wasn't exactly something she'd thought she'd be doing, should be doing, or even wanted to be doing.

"You know, the police probably bagged them; let's consider them lost in the abyss of evidence," suggested Harper. "I don't think we're ever going to find them."

Melissa turned on a heel, put her hands on her hips, and sassed, "Harper, dear, if you give up this way on everything that means something to you, do you think you'll ever make it as a painter?"

Brushing her hands off on her jeans, Harper took a deep breath and rolled her eyes to the ceiling, thinking how quickly the Melissa she knew all too well had so quickly come back. She shook her head back and forth.

"If you truly wish to help, then help find Connie," said Harper. "Meet me here, at the back door, tomorrow night. Dress as invisibly as possible. I've got an idea . . . it may be silly . . . but it might just work."

Melissa eyed the floor awkwardly, "I will be here if you believe it will help Miss Connie," she swallowed and dreaded the thought of anything happening to her Connie. She looked again to Harper with feigned confidence.

"Nine o'clock," reminded Harper. "Please don't be late."

With that, Melissa was gone.

Harper thought about the extraordinary evening she had just endured as she walked home, yet again trying to make sense of all that was not making sense.

Harper was determined to discover the truth about Connie's disappearance. The ordeal kept her awake in bed, tossing and turning, trying to solve the puzzle. She wasn't sure exactly how much sleep she got— four hours, maybe three? She didn't know for sure, but a renewed sense of purpose propelled her forward with borrowed energy.

Harper dragged herself back to the salon, now the scene of two crimes, possible murder, and, for sure, breaking and entering. She felt guilty for breaking into the salon the other night but believed it was for the greater good under the circumstances.

She now felt some compassion for Melissa; how sad for her to have mostly been alone in the special moments of her life. Thinking back, Harper could not recall her mother ever missing a school event, sporting competition, or to this day, their weekly afternoon tea. Harper had a new appreciation and felt grateful for her mother's tendency to 'hover.'

Cautiously guarded, she was satisfied with Melissa wanting to help. Finding out what happened to Connie was the most important thing right now, regardless of whether they despised each other. She felt good about this when Pearl entered the salon through the back door.

Her purse dangled precariously on her shoulder while she held two cups of to-go coffee. Pearl had to kick open the door and push it closed with her behind as she walked inside.

"Hey, Pearl!" called Harper from the salon floor. She placed a new boxed shipment of nail polishes by the acrylics station.

"Harper! Why, you're here so early, babe!" She seemed surprised to see Harper but smiled as she set her things down.

Harper noticed the two coffees, "Yeah, but you didn't have to bring me a coffee!"

Pearl laughed awkwardly and held one of the coffees out to her. "Early mornings, you know. Thought you could use a pick-me-up."

Harper eyed Pearl for a moment and took the coffee with gratitude. She wrapped her hands around the warm paper cup. The cup was flimsy as always because Minnie, who had the best coffee in town at her little cafe, would never spring for suitable paper cups. But Minnie never skimped on the quality of her coffee and always ground her beans fresh. Lifting the lid to her lips, Harper could smell the intoxicating dark roast with a touch of vanilla. "Ah, wonderful."

"So, Harper, ya here early to help with the big reopening?" Pearl sipped her coffee, then removed her jacket and tossed it onto a hook behind her.

Harper asked hesitantly, "We don't have a *big* reopening, do we? I mean, I thought we were just stocking everything that got ruined from the . . . blood."

"No, of course not," Pearl scoffed with a reassuring wave of her hand. "But the place opening back up *is* a big deal, don't you think?"

Without our Connie? Harper thought, feeling uncomfortable and sad. How could a hair competition exist without our Connie, or for that matter, The Curl Up and Dye?' Her head hurt from thinking so hard. She tried to smile, "Well, opening back up without Connie will be different, that's for sure."

CHAPTER 7

*M*elissa Montgomery first saw the teal leash in the dark. The rest of Harper Winslow materialized as she approached the familiar dog, dressed head to toe in all black.

"May I ask why we're sneaking around an alleyway?" Melissa asked the dark figure.

"Well, if the police aren't going to act accordingly, we'll just have to do the footwork our pretty little selves," Harper responded. "What in the name of cold beans are you wearing?"

Melissa scanned her ensemble. She wore gray yoga pants with a silver stripe going down each leg, a robin's-egg-blue hoodie displaying a fried egg (sunny side up), a wooly, gray sherpa cap (with pom), black satin gloves, and tan suede flats.

"You told me to wear my least fashionable clothes."

"I said your least *visible* clothes. And how are those shoes your least fashionable?"

"These are my only shoes without heels," replied the heiress.

"You don't own a pair of running shoes?"

"Oh, I never run. You can't possibly *make* me run." She looked at the crumpled cloth Harper was holding. "What exactly are we doing?"

Harper unfurled the cloth to reveal Connie's salon apron she had swiped from inside the shop, complete with its bedazzled 'C' monograms.

"We're going to track down Connie the old-fashioned way." Harper knelt to the ground and presented the apron to Beauregard, who sniffed it accordingly. "That's Miss Connie, Beau'. Can you smell her? Know the scent? We need to find her, boy. Help us find her, Beau!"

Her eyes adjusted to the low lighting; Melissa gestured toward the dog. "Um, has he *ever* done this before?"

"Once," replied Harper. "When I lost a pair of Chuck Taylors. I used my socks to trace them."

"And . . .?" inquired Melissa.

"And what?"

"Did he help you find them?"

"Of course," she replied. "Beau' led me right to them."

Melissa looked impressed. "Nice, very nice," she nodded approving.

Beauregard began rooting the ground like a bloodhound, moving zigzagged across the cold, dark pavement, stopping every few seconds to recover the scent.

"Mind you," added Harper, "he's the one who stole my Chucks in the first place."

"Oh! Here we go! He's picked something up!"

Beauregard was no longer zigzagging. His flappy little feet broke into a light jog as he led the two young ladies dressed as hoodlums down the dark alley behind downtown's shopping district. They were behind the bank. Then they were behind the Soup Fork Cafe. He stopped briefly at a dumpster behind the antique store and again at some discarded boxes outside Pullman Hardware. He'd perk his ears at the sound of unseen cars passing on the street or at something rattling on a far-off rooftop—maybe a wayward raccoon or alley cat. Then he would resume the search, his nose consistently low to the ground.

They crossed one street. Then another. Then a third.

Soon, they were within sight of the Dough Re Me's rear entrance and the fire escape of Harper's apartment. The girls were 'mall walking' now, practically running but in an awkward fashion.

"Isn't this where you live?" puffed Melissa, trying to breathe through what was likely the most exercise she'd had since high school gym class. She gestured toward the lit windows on the brick building's second story.

"Oh snap," replied Harper, also out of breath. "Looks like . . . I left the . . . lights on again," she huffed.

Beauregard was in a full-blown sprint, dragging the women behind a tight leash. He spotted a green paper bag in a nook at the conjunction of Green Acres and the funeral home. The aging but agile beagle homed in and ran straight to the bag. It had a 'Dough Re Me' logo and phone number on the side. Beauregard let out a low growl and then shoved his little face right into it.

"What'd ya find, boy? Is it a clue? Good boy, Beau!" Harper bent over to look closely.

Beauregard withdrew his snout, munching something and making a mess, then looked up to Harper, visibly pleased.

"I don't think he's found our Connie," Melissa bent over and picked up the green to-go bag with its brown spindled handles. "For Pete's sake!" she sighed, frustrated, and displayed the available contents to her cohort.

"Buttered scones," Harper replied while rolling her eyes. "Of course." Melissa was less than enthused, "I guess you can't teach an old dog new tricks after all," she raised the bag closer to her face and looked inside. "But wait, there *is* something else." She reached into the bag and withdrew a small silver tube.

"What is *that*?" Harper asked.

"Hard to tell in this light," Melissa held the tube closer to her eyes, trying to read the label. "Costume adhesive, it says."

"Costume adhesive is not exactly my idea of a go-to condiment," Harper chuckled, "especially for scones!" She leaned over to cuddle and kiss her four-legged buddy, "Way to go, Beau' my silly sleuth!"

CHAPTER 8

$\mathcal{H}$arper decided this weekend might become one of her favorites, especially considering the whirlwind of events. She spent her Saturday morning lounging on the couch with Beauregard, and now, for her Saturday evening, she had dressed in a slim-fitting, silvery skirt with a slit up the side, making her feel put-together for once. She left the house, hair up in a bun and jean jacket around her shoulders, kissed Beauregard goodbye, and ventured out.

With butterflies in her tummy and anticipation she could hardly contain, Harper decided to maintain confidence. Tonight was going to be some night.

SHE ARRIVED at the gallery building just as the golden rays of sunlight set on the horizon. The sky was clear and bright. Scattered stars were beginning to poke through the darkening twilight veil.

Charlotte had purchased the building for her new gallery on a corner street next to a small French boutique. One had to enter the building through the boutique, walking past luxurious offerings toward the back counter and arriving at a second set of massive glass doors. Harper oogled over the cashmere scarfs and leather bags along the entrance but swiftly reached the gallery doors.

Passing through the heavy entry, Harper paused to take in the impressive gallery layout, a chic, open space with exposed brick walls, high ceilings, and many windows for natural light. A spiral black wrought iron staircase in one corner led up to a loft where paintings lay in wait, ready to be sold or shipped to their future homes.

Men in service liveries—complete with tails and white gloves—glided through the magnificent room, precariously balancing gold platters of champagne flutes equally precarious and filled to their brims.

The champagne bubbles shimmered gold beneath the soft chandelier lights, casting scattered sparkly patterns across the dark, cherry-stained wood floors. Harper also sparkled in her borrowed drop earrings and long, shimmering skirt, which she carefully lifted as she entered the soiree'.

Harper was already admiring the eclectic variety of local pieces from the entrance—impressionist, abstract, minimalist, regionalist, hyperrealist oil, watercolors, collage, and plaster relief. The display was a cross-section of modern Central Virginia art culture reflecting its long and storied past. Charlotte had truly outdone herself in renovating the place. Impressive.

The evening air was already boozy. The room brimmed with all the socialites of Emerson, mingling, schmoozing, and gossiping ears off as they eyed up and down the various exhibits while sipping drinks. Local trendsetters, politicians, and community bigwigs enjoyed the finest art and spirits.

A server offered Harper a silver tray of champagne flutes. She graciously took her bubbly beverage and promptly gulped down half of it.

"Thirsty," she said to the stunned, wide-eyed server, smacking her lips in fizzy satisfaction. The bubbly tingle went straight to her head.

"Nice tux," she added and strolled away.

I need to find my partner-in-crime, or I should say partner-in-solving-crime! Listen to me, thought Harper, I'm considering Melissa my partner! It's a bit hard to stomach, but I'm willing to go with it if we can clear up this disaster!

Thinking of Melissa as anything other than a mean girl was a challenge. Who would have ever thought the day would come when she felt caring or concerned for Melissa? It was just then Harper felt a hand frantically patting her shoulder. She spun around to see Melissa looking stunned and freaked out.

"Melissa! Welcome to the party! You don't exactly look festive! My goodness, I mean, have you looked in a mirror? Your dress is gorgeous, but you're looking a bit terrified. Are you OK?"

"I'm just nervous!" Melissa's frightful expression faded long enough for her to shrug coyly and touch the fabric of her soft pink dress, the bodice entirely made of tulle. "I dressed for the occasion," she leaned down in her six-inch heels, making Harper feel very short, "and look, I can stash three pairs of binoculars in this bra."

Harper almost spit out her champagne. "What do we need binoculars for? We're not spies!"

Melissa looked anxious again. "I'm sorry, OK? As I said, I'm just nervous! I've never gone undercover! And how much different is undercover from being a spy? I didn't like sneaking into the Curl Up the other night—it made my stomach queasy; oh, Harper, this stuff isn't my cup of tea!"

Again, Harper laughed. "We're not going undercover, you goof. We are just working the room; all we want is info, something to help us out, and your job is to cozy up to Charlotte. Learn everything you can. Find out what she knows."

"Like where was *she* on the night of Connie's disappearance, right?"

"Exactly. I'll see if that curator friend of hers is around. She's bound to know something, too."

Melissa shrugged. Harper thought she looked like a lost, frightened kitten in Dior. Before offering further encouragement, they overheard greetings from the crowded room as Charlotte glided through the sea of guests, artists, and admirers.

Melissa turned to look and immediately spun back around, her expression blank and her face turning white from nerves.

Harper was impatient with Melissa, "We don't have time for this, missy; snap out of it!"

They were wasting valuable time, and this night was so important! Harper started to imagine her mother's voice, a parental voice telling her to be kind and not to be rude. Harper planted both hands firmly on Melissa's shoulders, looking her straight in the eye. "Look, I'll be here the entire time, watching. We can do this. You can do this. Charlotte is harmless, anyway."

"Then why in the world are we talking to her?" hissed Melissa, her tone changed to that of a panicked mouse.

"If there's even the slightest chance that Charlotte had something to do with Connie's disappearance, it's worth talking to her, that's why. You said yourself that she was hounding Connie about buying her salon.

Well, what if she *did* have something to do with Connie missing so the building might become available for her to buy?"

"Wow," Melissa was stunned by the idea, "well, you may be on to something. The Curl Up and Dye has one of the best spots in town." Still, her nerves were at an all-time high, so when she turned around to "casually" stroll off in search of Charlotte, she nearly bumped into a server carrying a tray of petit fours.

Harper watched Melissa stumble around the room like a ping-pong ball. She began to realize that her witty arch nemesis with the snarky bite and perfect skin was simply putty under pressure, an utterly chaotic mess of nerves.

After a few more sips of champagne, Melissa located Charlotte and awkwardly followed her around the room. She was ducking, weaving, and sneaking glances through and between the crooks of high society elbows. Until this very moment, Harper would never have believed Melissa Montgomery could even break a sweat. But here she was, glistening under the soft chandeliers hanging throughout the gallery.

As amused as Harper was, she felt like Melissa could blow their cover. Watching, she looked over towards the curator, Charlotte's good friend and business partner, Maureen. Maureen was equally as well-known as Charlotte, having curated exhibits nationwide. For her to be in a tiny town like Emerson piqued curiosity, and Harper couldn't help but wonder what the locale fare could offer this duo.

She thought Melissa's anxious behavior would raise suspicion and needed to intervene. Harper made a beeline straight for the two curators.

She caught up just as Melissa obnoxiously cleared her throat to garner Harper's attention.

"Charlotte!" Harper threw her arms around the tall blonde in an excitable hug. She smiled and stood awkwardly, folding and unfolding her arms, trying to find the most casual posture. She appreciated the encounter with Charlotte, anything to corral Melissa, who was ghost-white and had already finished a third glass of champagne.

"You're here! Oh, Harper, I'm so glad!" Charlotte exclaimed with a broad grin. "Welcome to the newest edition of our future, a string of art galleries across the south! Next month's gallery event will be all about you showing *your* work! What do you think?

"My humble finger paintings? Shown here? I'll say!" Harper glanced around the room, "I think this is a beautiful space, a place with ceilings reaching to the sky and the fanciest glassware I've ever seen, and yet it still feels so cozy."

"Yeah, what'd you pay for it?!" Melissa slurred quite loudly.

Harper heard Melissa and cringed; my gosh, have some manners, Melissa! Blank faces turned toward the slurred, loud voice to stare at a very tipsy Melissa, who immediately realized her classless faux pas. She pursed her lips and sipped more champagne, hoping to smooth over the moment.

"Melissa's father owns a chocolate factory," Harper blurted out instinctively, attempting to justify the awkward comment, "and she wants to . . . um, open a store, so she is wondering about the market rates."

"Exactly," Melissa jumped in and added, "Daddy says a little shop about this size, selling all of the latest in luxurious chocolates, would be perfect for Emerson." The girls knew not to even look at one another.

Charlotte shifted her glance between them. "Oh, I see," then she chuckled, "Well," clearing her throat, "it wasn't cheap, darlings."

Harper and Melissa chuckled awkwardly along with Charlotte until a distinguished-looking little man in a suit approached, holding a small, gold-rimmed plate of half-eaten dessert and claiming to be a woodworker specializing in art frames. Another man arrived shortly after, greeting her warmly as an old friend and asking how the family was.

More and more guests greeted Charlotte, complimenting the woman of the hour, congratulating her on the opening, and taking the attention entirely away from Melissa and Harper. "Thank goodness," sighed Harper.

"Sorry, loves, everyone wants a piece of me tonight!" Charlotte was beaming and giggling before returning to another complimentary conversation, leaving Harper and Melissa to stand there.

Mission failed for the moment. So far, nothing.

Melissa discouraged, took advantage of the server, walking around with a platter of triple chocolate pie slices. Through a mouthful of whipped cream, she sighed and gave Harper puppy-dog eyes. Harper was sure Melissa wanted to leave and decided to seek out the other curator. "Let's go find Maureen." Melissa reluctantly agreed. Making their way, guest after guest detained them, asking questions. Everyone wanted to know what was happening. Everyone wondered about the whereabouts of Connie.

Harper was astounded by some guests and their offensive questioning. Harper *particularly* enjoyed being asked if *she* was the murderer and had chopped Connie into pieces. Nice. Also, if there would be a funeral and if she had "saved some relic of the crime for a magic ritual to find out Connie's whereabouts." This from a flamboyant little old lady with a strong scent of lilac, grinning excitedly at the idea.

The emotional weight was taking its toll and becoming quite the burden to the amateur sleuths.

Harper was circulating in the room one last lap and nearly collided with Gabriel, who seemed to appear out of thin air. Wearing a white chef's jacket and carrying a tray of individually plated triple chocolate pie slices, he smiled and balanced his goodie tray.

"Whoa! In a rush?" Harper joked, putting her hands up to stop their collision. Pretty sure her ruby cheeks had betrayed her, she quickly stepped around him so he could continue, but Gabriel stayed in the way; he gave Harper a look-over. Her fingertips lightly brushed against him, and she put her hands down immediately, blushing at the buzz of being so close to him.

"I should ask *you* what's the rush," retorted Gabriel, steadying the platter.

Harper laughed breathlessly and gestured past him to the gallery floor, where Melissa was standing next to a large, bright abstract painting, quietly picking at her nails.

"My friend is having a small crisis," Harper noticed his attire, "I didn't realize you were catering this event!"

"Yeah," Gabriel shrugged. "I do it on the side. It's a good source of added income for the bakery. Would you like a dessert?"

Harper quickly let him know before he could pick up a small plate and hand it to her. "No, thanks! Gotta get back out there."

Gabriel nodded, and with a quick smile, Harper was off again, headed for the main gallery room.

Melissa knew Gabriel wanted to talk; given different circumstances, she would have enjoyed his company. But time was of the essence.

Melissa was nowhere to be found, not in any direction. Harper frantically searched for her through the crowd of partygoers. Behind several suits and dresses mingling, Harper finally spotted her; Melissa was standing in front of Charlotte, leaning in close, eyes burning a hole right through Charlotte's and by the look on her face, confusing her.

Harper could hardly believe what she saw next. Melissa grabbed a butter knife from Charlotte's plate and stabbed it through a sepia-toned lithograph of a plantation homestead.

She gasped! The room gasped, and many more appalled gasps were audible throughout the crowd.

Harper shoved people to the floor, sprinting to reach Melissa, who stared in stunned surprise. She allowed Harper to link her arm and gently pull her off to the side of the room, far away from the destroyed painting and Charlotte, who had released a blood-curdling scream.

Gripping the painting as if it were a child, "You've ruined a one-of-a-kind piece! Do you know how much this is worth?!" Charlotte was screaming after her.

They could hear her screams as they exited, running through the boutique shop. Harper steered Melissa, who was still in too much shock to speak. They burst through the front doors and into the fresh, open air.

The night was crisp, and Melissa sucked in massive breaths of fresh air while Harper patted her hand sympathetically. Unable to calm her, Melissa lurched over, losing her dinner in the bushes.

"I can't believe I just did what I did!"

Harper rubbed circles on her back reassuringly. "It's my fault," Harper sighed. "I shouldn't have pushed you to help me. You have sipped too much bubbly to calm your nerves, and you had a bit of an uncontrolled moment in there."

Melissa kept on. "I *stabbed* a painting! I'm a complete psychopath! If anyone discovers those were *my* shears in the Curl Up, they'll banish me from town. It'll be over for me! And now I go and do this thoughtless outburst. I don't exactly look innocent!" Her voice was shaking, and she squeaked out a small sob.

"I'll talk to Charlotte. I'll explain. I'll say . . . something."

"What? What could you say? That I came down with a sudden bout of something or a panic attack?" Melissa was hysterical, and Harper was dismayed. Melissa had lost it, and taking her frustration out by stabbing a painting? It probably *was* a panic attack.

"We'll think of something, Melissa." She gave her one last shoulder pat before they decided it best to head home.

Harper had planned on walking home after the soiree' and brought a pair of sneakers in a bag. Melissa slipped her heels off her bare, aching feet, then decided walking was absurd and called her private driver. Harper typically would never accept an offer from Melissa for a lift. The mere idea of spending any time other than necessary with Melissa, especially in a small, confined space, seemed impossible.

This time, she took her up on her offer graciously, and the two women spent the short ride to Harper's apartment comparing blisters and preparing a conversation to smooth everything over with Charlotte.

CHAPTER 9

The next day, at the salon, Harper found Detectives Boychester and Mumford sipping from styrofoam cups that looked tiny in their large, rough hands. They were talking to Pearl.

"Now, Miss Pearl, we are doin' all we can, and if you'd kindly unhand me, I could explain."

Pearl's tiny grasp was tight around Detective Boychester's arm, but Pearl wasn't threatening him. She was staring up at him with wide, bright googly eyes. When Harper walked in, she thought she saw her irises turn to hearts momentarily. Harper thought for sure Pearl was smitten with Detective Boychester.

"Do you work out much?" asked Pearl in a dreamy voice. "In your uniform, perhaps?"

Detective Boychester looked entirely uncomfortable and cleared his throat.

"Well, sometimes I jog in a matching velour tracksuit that belongs to my wife."

At the mention of 'wife,' Pearl groaned and rolled her eyes, releasing the man and allowing circulation to flow back to his extremities.

Detective Mumford was also busy with one of the ladies of the salon. The technician was practicing her French tip technique *on him!* Harper's mom, Georgia, was also there, watching and, by the grin on her face, quite amused!

Detective Boychester announced, "We need to get down to business. Ah, Harper Winslow, just the face I was lookin' for!"

"How are you, Detective?" asked Harper as she sat her bag down and shrugged off her jean jacket. By the looks of faces around her, she could tell there had been some heavy questioning going on, or at least plenty of attempts. Thwarted by Pearl's flirtatious mood or the nail tech's eagerness to practice her craft, the unsuspecting Muffins, now sitting there, had three glossy, French-tipped nails two inches longer than the rest.

"I'll be better after you tell me how your evening went last night. Heard it was *quite eventful*," Detective Boychester directed his comments to Harper, giving her a look of suspicion. He tucked his thumbs into the front of his belt and puffed out his chest a bit. She briefly thought he resembled a bird trying to make himself appear bigger in front of a potential threat.

"It was a casual evening," she replied with a casual shrug. She told herself there was nothing to worry about, even Melissa going rabid on a painting.

"Heard you were schmoozin' with the high class," offered Muffins, placing a hand on his hip. His new set of nails had given him a sudden source of sassy confidence, and he walked over to a nearby counter, picked up a pair of shears, and held them up. "We heard someone got *violent*," he flipped the shears casually over in his palm. It was hard to take him seriously with his 'practice nails' on the hand holding the scissors.

"We heard you two were whisperin' to each other all night, huddled up together like a couple of quarterbacks makin' a play," added Detective Boychester. His head bobbed up and down as he burned a hole into her eyes, expecting a full admission.

Harper looked at them, her gaze switching between them as they stood there. Both looked down at her like she was doing something wrong, just staring back. It got uncomfortable and intimidating, a stare-down between the three; Harper finally sighed and relented, at least somewhat.

"She had a bad moment," Harper said, "maybe just talk to her."

"Oh, we plan on it," said Boychester in a long, drawn-out southern drawl. He flipped his sunshades, sitting atop his head down, and looked at his partner. "Muffins, let's roll."

The two were gone as quickly as they'd arrived, out the door in a whirlwind of paisley business ties and ill-fitting suits. The second the door closed and the bells stopped jingling, the room exploded with gab.

They chatted like it was their favorite pastime.

Paulette and Claudette, who had been under the bonnet dryers the entire time, were giggling to each other about Pearl's 'romantic encounter, one to rival the greatest Harlequin romance novels,' Pearl was sitting behind the front desk, chatting away to Jenna and Georgia about all the tough questioning.

"Did you hear him ask me if I had ever been to the 'bad part of town?'" Pearl leaned across the desk, elbows propped up on the table as she rested her chin in her hands.

"Doesn't he realize that there is no such thing as a bad part of town in our area?" quipped Georgia. "Even the seediest bar is located in the next quaint little town over!" They both cackled together and decided to visit the bar for some drinks that weekend.

Georgia even joked, "Maybe they'll find some trash on the street and report their scandalous discovery in the so-called 'bad part' of town to the detectives." Their laughter continued.

Amidst the discussions of the morning's eventful happenings, Harper took a moment to send messages to Gabriel and Melissa requesting a meet-up. Both of them responded promptly. Gabriel mentioned that he was occupied with work at the bakery all day but invited them to join him there, offering an abundance of pumpkin cream cheese muffins for the taking.

Once the sun had set, Harper descended from her apartment after spending seven hours sketching for her upcoming art exhibit. Downstairs, she found Gabriel in his customary white apron, with his face half covered in flour, kneading a giant ball of dough on the floured surface of a counter.

"Hey, save some of that flour for the dough," teased Harper, pointing to his cheek where a big swipe of flour was highlighting his left cheekbone. Gabriel smirked back at her and lifted a corner of his apron to wipe it away.

"Careful, or you won't get those pumpkin muffins," Gabriel teased back before playfully flicking a speck of flour at Harper, who jumped back and laughed in surprise. "Where's your friend, anyway?"

"She's right here," an all-too-familiar voice piped up by the front door. Melissa wore sunglasses and the same wide-brimmed, floppy sunhat Harper encountered that night at the salon. She wore an oversized coat that rivaled the size and shapelessness of the previous one she wore as a disguise. Her demeanor was straightforward. She purposely dressed this way.

She glanced around the bakery, wary of any potential eyes or ears, but the bakery was already closed.

"Mel, why are you wearing sunglasses at night? And take off that stupid coat. This gathering isn't an underground Illuminati meeting," Harper beckoned her over.

"Right, no Illuminati, they live inside the moon," Gabriel quipped.

"Oh, so, I'm 'Mel' now?" Melissa ignored Gabriel's moon comment and moved behind the front counters. She removed her sunglasses and looked around at all the delicious freshly baked goods. "It smells like bread in this place," she said, nose turned up.

"It's a bakery," said Gabriel.

The trio stood around the long, butcher-block island beneath the soft spotlight hanging above them. Their gathering was unofficial but felt like the backdrop for an inquisition. The smell of bread was their only lingering comfort.

"So, why have we all gathered here today?" asked Gabriel, his tone lined with sarcasm, and Harper shot him a withering stare.

"Because the detectives came to the Curl Up this morning, asking a lot of questions," explained Harper. "I think *they think* Melissa and I are . . . I don't know, conspiring or guilty of something."

Melissa nervously cleared her throat before informing them of her encounter with the bumbling, half-wit detectives. "I spent the afternoon down at the police station," she said, glancing at Harper.

"What?!" exclaimed Harper in panic, "you hadn't mentioned. Did they ask about us at the gallery opening?"

"Yes," Melissa replied, nodding and adding, "They asked about you, too, Gabriel."

"Me? But they had already stopped by the bakery. I told them I was in the back the entire time, working in the kitchen. I must have plated about three hundred of those pie slices," he shook his head in disbelief.

"Oh, but it was *so* good," piped up Melissa, gushing over the dessert, which garnered much attention during the evening. "Did you use cinnamon in the crust? Genius. My family's chef uses cardamom, and I find it so undignified."

"Oh, I didn't make it," Gabriel stated. "She had a friend who wanted to help cut the cost of having a caterer. She let her make the pies. I think she may be one of your pals at the salon; her name was . . .Paula, I think.

"Paula? I *think*?" questioned Melissa sarcastically.

"Pearl? Maybe?" asked Harper, her mind wandering to the dessert, realizing she didn't get to try it. Her intake had primarily been that of alcohol and bubbly carbonation.

"Yeah, Pearl, that was it," he replied, wagging a finger and pouting, "I still don't know why she'd hire a baker if she didn't want me to bake anything. Dessert is, like, half my repertoire!"

"You don't say..." Harper said faintly.

CHAPTER 10

$\mathcal{I}$t was supposed to be the week of Harper's first art exhibit, and the case of figuring out what happened to Connie was still unsolved.

Harper reached out to Charlotte and apologized for the erratic behavior displayed by her friend, blaming it on a sour glass of champagne.

After Charlotte made Harper promise to keep all sharp objects out of her friend Melissa's hands during the exhibit (and pay handsomely for the damages), they were back to business.

Harper had planned to arrive early on the day of the show with a truck bed loaded with completed paintings. She felt relieved that she had enough pieces for her prospective exhibit, but she still needed the job of a hair stylist to secure her space in the gallery after the show.

She was in a tough situation. Her boutique would not generate enough revenue to cover the rent, and she needed to find a way to make ends meet. She was worried about failing once again, this time on her plan to partner with the gallery as a boutique owner. She was desperate to find a solution and was even trying to locate Connie to help fix everything.

Harper couldn't imagine the humiliation of a gallery failure, "I'd be a one-hit wonder, open and closing on the same day."

GEORGIA SURPRISED her daughter with a spontaneous shopping trip to their favorite boutique, where they found bejeweled bracelets and the perfect jeans for Harper's slender legs.

The French accordion music playing softly in the background added to the cozy boutique atmosphere. Harper was browsing through a collection of leather handbags when she told her mother about Charlotte's inquiry regarding the exhibit she was working on. "She said she's excited to see them, but I'm nervous," Harper fixed a crooked bag on its hook.

Georgia made a "pfft!" sound. "You'll be fabulous, and they'll be fabulous. You'll sell them all! And I'm buying the first one."

Smiling, Harper glanced at the front door, watching as a middle-aged woman in a deep green pea coat walked in, looking flustered from the wind raging outside. The weather in Emerson had been chaotic that day, and everyone who entered seemed positively windswept.

Amused by all the pushed-back, puffed-out hairdos she'd seen that day, Harper was staring off, lost in deep thought, and hadn't realized the deep green pea coat person with the windswept hair was standing right behind her. Georgia cleared her throat. "ahem...."

"Oh!" Harper, startled, spun around, coming nose-to-nose with the woman, who grinned brightly behind oversized bone-rimmed glasses and enough makeup to repaint the state of Virginia.

"Shug!" the pea coat woman exclaimed, looking joyful and enthused to see Harper.

Harper squinted, puzzled, flipping through her memories to figure out how she *knew* this woman, and then it clicked! She *looked* like Connie and even *spoke* like Connie, albeit faster and louder.

"You're Connie's younger sister!" Harper exclaimed.

"Well, yaas, and you're the girl I've been seein' all over the news. Yep, I'm the little sister, I sure am! Proud of it, too. Connie was so successful, what with her business and all—well, I don't want to say '*was*' quite yet. I saw you here and wanted to come over and meet the last person to see my big sis alive," she gave Harper a smile that made her stomach feel uneasy.

As she walked around a rack of clothes, Georgia introduced herself. She extended her hand for a handshake. "Well, now, I'm Georgia, Harper's mother, pleasure to make your acquaintance," she said with some protective tone.

"Pleasure, Georgia, I'm Hillie," replied the woman, taking Georgia's hand and shaking it daintily as if Georgia's fingers were a used tissue.

"So, you live in town?" asked Georgia, drawing her hand back and placing it in her coat pocket, the other following suit.

"Oh, goodness, no! I could never leave the city. I came home when I heard Connie went missin', and I've been hounding the news stations and posting flyers ever since."

Harper's mouth fell open a bit in surprise. That's *where I recognize her from*, she thought. Harper had seen a Hillie Clark on her city's local news, sobbing and begging Connie to "please come home!"

"So expensive, the flyers! Do you know how much printer ink costs?" Hillie continued, "And the gas I've gone through driving around, tacking them all up! Of course, I'm not complaining, anything for my sister Connie."

Harper and Georgia exchanged glances, silently judging the sanity of "Hillie" knowing they were both thinking the same thing.

Hillie continued without waiting for a response.

"You know, I looked up the cost of funerals in Emerson. You only have one funeral parlor in this town! Did you know that? I'm sure that's why the owner charges such ridiculous prices! Eight thousand dollars for a casket, honestly? We don't even have a body. What does he expect me to put in it, my tears?" Hillie wiped her tears.

"My goodness, maybe a few keepsakes?" offered Harper.

"No, no, Hillie, we're not thinking about a funeral, not anytime soon," Georgia wanted to change the subject.

She put her arm gently around Harper's shoulders and pulled her closer seeing her daughter was clearly rattled by Hillie's brashness and callous demeanor regarding her own sister. "Harper, honey, the police are still heavily investigating."

Hillie cackled, replying, "Of course, I haven't *planned* a funeral. . . well, you know, its just with everything…I've been wondering... who's caring for the salon while my sister is gone?"

Another exchange of glances, but this time Harper spoke up first. "Oh, that's Pearl. She's the manicurist, head assistant, accountant, secretary, front desk . . . she does a lot of everything. She's a big help to Connie."

"Especially now, I'm sure," inserted Hillie. Her tone of voice had developed a slightly bitter edge. Sensing her shift in the conversation, Georgia spoke up.

"Well, I need to get my daughter home. She's got a big show coming up, and she must prepare." Georgia, pushing her hand against the small of her daughter's back, prompted her to head for the exit.

"Right!" agreed Harper quickly, more than happy to escape this nightmarish conversation. "So much work to get done. Nice to meet you!"

"See you on the news," said Hillie, waving farewell to them both as they left, a snarky smile plastered across her face.

It took three cups of coffee, a round from the ice cream parlor, and the honking of oncoming traffic before Harper snapped out of her trance. Georgia tossed their empty to-go cups into a sidewalk bin before hugging her daughter goodbye outside the ice cream parlor.

"Don't fret, hon. Your art needs you now, and don't be bulldozed by that woman. Go paint your heart out and get your mind off Connie; it will be good for you. I've got my nail appointment."

Harper heard her mother, but her head was not filled with many thoughts. She could only think about their odd encounter with Connie's sister. Hillie. Hillie. Hillie.

She pivoted impulsively and piped up to her mother, "Can I tag along, mama, to The Curl Up and Dye? I can grab a nail appointment while your have yours? I'll get some fresh color. I don't think I could focus on my painting just yet."

Georgia linked arms with her, replying delightedly, "Of course you can! How about we pick matching nail polish, a color to match what you plan to wear for your first big art exhibit? We'll need photos, lots of photos, with all your paintings!"

Georgia chattered excitedly about the exhibit the entire way over to the salon. "What is the color palette of your collection? I don't want to "clash with the background." Her mother's concerns amused Harper.

Harper had her fair share of concerns; her desperate need to work, mixed guilt about Connie, and her burning desire to fulfill her artistic dream. She tried desperately to be present and enjoy the opportunity for a little break instead of the worries tugging at her insides.

Knowing her mother would insist on helping her financially, Harper had to keep her plan to herself if she were to attain her goal of absolute independence.

Once inside the salon, Harper went straight to the break room, feigning a desperate need for a drink. It wasn't *entirely* untrue—she was jonesing for a cup of fresh hot coffee. She needed something to help her get through what she was about to do.

The door to Connie's office was in the break room between a sink that never had consistent hot water and a stack of boxes full of shampoo. It was tiny and held only a small desk with a computer chair and plenty of current magazines. And in the desk drawers, as Harper would soon find, were all of Connie's bills and mail, some unopened. Underneath a layer of old love letters from days gone by were the inner workings of Connie's salon, correspondence, sales flyers, and bills—lots of bills.

She saw several disconnect notices stamped with a disapproving, bright red 'OVERDUE' on the front. It was shocking to see so many unpaid. Underneath a disconnect notice for water, Harper found a single blank envelope. It needed addressing and a stamp but held a letter inside. Someone did not seal it either, and Harper reasoned, with a heavy helping of guilt, that her nosiness was for a good cause.

She reached into the envelope and pulled out the letter. She gasped out loud. It was a will! A *signed* will, citing in plain words that Connie would, upon her death, leave everything to—

"Harper?" Georgia's voice interrupted the moment and sent panicked chills down Harper's spine. She jumped, shoved all the papers back into the drawer, and pushed it closed, careful not to slam it and make noise.

She hurried out of the office and, shutting the door behind her, Harper took a moment to breathe. Then, gathering herself, she walked around the corner and onto the salon floor, where the ladies were doing business as usual.

"There she is! The artist!" exclaimed Georgia, tossing her hands up from where she sat, head tilted slightly back as Pearl stood behind her, misting it with water.

"Hopefully not starving artist," commented Pearl, looking at Harper hard. "You eaten today, hon? You look a little peaked."

Harper didn't answer. Since opening The Curl Up and Dye, Pearl had been Connie's accountant, best friend, and right-hand woman. Based on the number of disconnect notices, she should be doing her job now in these categories.

"Pearl? Can I talk to you?" Harper asked somewhat meekly. Pearl looked up from behind the register and scheduling book.

"Sure, babe. Are you OK? Because you look a little pale," she walked out from behind the front counter and placed a cool hand on Harper's forehead. "You don't feel warm or anything."

"I'm fine," said Harper, tilting her head away from the intruding hand thermometer. "Pearl, did you know about the will?"

Pearl's face, wearing a pleasant smile, suddenly drained of all color and expression, replaced with blank shock. Harper, studying her facial expression, felt hurt. "You knew! You knew she'd left her entire business to her sister, and you didn't tell the Detectives?" Pearl could hear the strain in Harper's voice.

She took Harper's hands and gave them a gentle squeeze. "Harper! Harper, babe, you don't need to concern yourself with Hillie Clark! That woman ain't but a strong odor in the wind; she's harmless!"

"But I ran into her, and she was talking about funeral and poster expenses, and—" Harper stuttered, trailing off the end of her sentence. She was baffled. Why hadn't Pearl gone to the police and turned in the will? Why hadn't the police searched Connie's office? Maybe they didn't get inside. Perhaps they just left it

111

and didn't go in. Harper had found it challenging to wedge her small frame between the sink and boxes to get inside.

Pearl continued trying to ease her fears. "Hillie's just greedy, that's all! Connie wrote that will *years ago*. I didn't give it another thought," she shrugged.

Something seemed off for Harper; something was not fitting. She silently turned away and walked back into the break room.

Sounds of the fridge and cabinet drawers opening and slamming shut came from the break room. Harper reemerged, holding a plate with a fork and a single slice of pie in the middle. She held it out to Pearl, who had come out from behind the front counter and stood on the salon floor, looking back at her blankly. "What's this, hon?" asked Pearl.

"This," began Harper in a loud voice for all to hear, "*this* is the pie served at Charlotte's gallery opening, triple chocolate pie slices. Where did *you* get it from?"

The room exchanged glances of confusion. Wondering about the severe tone in her questioning; Harper had commanded the room's attention, especially Georgia, who stood from her chair and looked worriedly at her daughter.

"Harper," she said. "What's going on, honey?"

Pearl went on, "It's store-bought, babe, like always. I picked it up from Minnie's grocery this morning."

Harper shook her head and scoffed. "No, there's no way. This pie tastes exactly like Connie's! It looks exactly like Connie's, too! This is not store-bought!"

Pearl sighed and walked over to Harper, running a comforting hand down her arm. "That's just 'cause Connie *always got the store-bought*, sweet pea."

"Whaaat?!" Harper's head was swimming. She couldn't wrap her head around what she heard, "... store bought...no... this *was* Connie's pie."

"What about the coffee?" she asked suddenly.

"What? What coffee? Hon, you're not making any sense," said Pearl.

Harper practically screamed. "The coffee! You brought *two* coffees that early morning, and I knew it wasn't for me! You didn't know I'd be there!"

"Now, Harper . . ." started Pearl, putting a hand up defensively. "You need to calm down."

"What did you *do* to her?" demanded Harper, squaring off with Pearl.

Before things got worse, the bells on the front door jingled; a moment later, Melissa appeared in the foyer, looking in on the awkward confusion. It was clear that she had stepped into the middle of something dire.

113

She noticed the plate of pie Harper was gripping, the flesh of her thumb turning white from her grip; Melissa's expression brightened, and she licked her lips. "Ooh, pie! I just had a croissant, but I don't mind if I do! It... looks...so familiar!"

"Doesn't it?" Harper snipped, and Melissa looked puzzled. "Don't eat it," she commanded, giving Pearl an accusatory look. "You don't know what's in it."

Pearl tossed her hands up in the air and scoffed loudly. "You are being *ridiculous*, Harper!" Her insistence made Harper's blood boil.

"Harper!" Melissa cut in, "What is going on here?"

Harper could not talk. Not now, not there. She placed the pie plate on the nearest chair and took Melissa by her arm, ushering her towards the door. She glanced at her mother, hoping she might understand she was acting with purpose.

"I'll explain everything, Mel, let's get to the bakery."

CHAPTER 11

*O*n the day of Harper's art exhibition, the weather matched the mood; dreary. Rain was forecasted all week, proving local weatherman Maxwell Freeze was correct. Harper tossed a heavy tarp over her paintings after loading them into the bed of her mother's pickup truck, which Georgia used to haul large gardening pots and landscaping bricks.

She started the morning bringing twenty-seven paintings, ranging from large to massive in scale, to the gallery. By early evening, the thundering rain had died down to a drizzle. It was all Harper could do to maintain her poise for the day. Her nerves were on high alert anticipating whether she would have a successful show, and she could not shake the thought of her artwork bombing with the patrons.

If she is not a success this evening, she imagined the worst; besides the social humiliation, she would hang up her paintbrushes, most likely for good. "I'll be another creative statistic," thought Harper out loud, "and won't my mother have much to say about this round of failure."

She looked around the gallery. Well, *this part* of the evening is all set; now I've got to swing back home to take care of the rest.

Harper waited in the bakery, staring at the fading "CLOSED" sign hanging in the windowed door. She was anxious and focused on relaxing, sitting patiently at the counter until Gabriel appeared in the doorway. He had agreed to be her date for the exhibit *and,* after confidently hammering out many details together, decided to help with her *other goal* for the evening. She felt such appreciation for his support; he was a good friend.

Still wearing her lace fringed cocktail dress, her *'not-my-date'* approached, looking quite handsome, still smelling like cinnamon; she noticed him holding a muffin. She could smell the baked cinnamon; my favorite, she thought, yep, an excellent friend.

"Mmmh, my fav is cinnamon," she giggled, looking up at him. Yep, so far, he was an excellent 'not-my-date.'

The art gallery was as elegant as always and full of partygoers looking to drink champagne, schmooze, and talk about art like seasoned scholars.

The second Harper walked in, the gossiping started spinning. She was arm in arm with Gabriel, with his perfectly fitting tuxedo and faint pleasant cinnamon bakery aroma. The last art gallery event was still on guests' minds; whispers whirled of whether Melissa Montgomery would show up and "cause a scene again."

Harper tried to ignore the talk and focus on her big night. She was excited and in a better mood than she had been in weeks. She even allowed her mother to pick up Beauregard and bring him. He would fit right in with a faux-diamond leash attached to his new collar, sporting an elegant, black tulle bow that covered half his face. He didn't mind; he seemed to strut a little prouder in his doggy finery.

While standing with Gabriel, Georgia introduced herself and told him she once ordered a delicious three-tier cake from his bakery, much to Gabriel's amusement. Harper looked over the room for her friends and kept an eye out for Pearl.

Charlotte broke her line of sight, appearing in front of her wearing a large, cherry-red smile. She came right over through the crowd. Squeezing Harper in a hug of excitement, Charlotte practically lifted her off her heels. "Your first big exhibit!" she squealed, looking at Georgia and dropping her mouth open exaggeratedly, "Georgia! How excited are we?"

"The pieces are fantastic," Georgia said with a grin.

"I agree, Georgia! So, Harper," Charlotte turned to her friend, "here's the plan. In a bit, I'll gather everyone around your main focal piece, introduce you, and then you'll give a little speech—nothing major, no biggie, right?"

"Umm, sure, OK."

"Great!"

Charlotte turned and flounced off to greet her guests and direct a small gaggle of servers to wander with trays of hors d'oeuvres.

Beginning to panic about her speech, Harper looked at her mom. "Oh, I am not looking forward to this part." She buried her face in her mother's shoulder.

"You'll do just fine," assured her mother, kissing her on her head. Then she looked at Gabriel, adding with a wink, "You have friends to support you here, like her," he pointed behind them, and they spotted Melissa across the room.

Catching Harper's eye, Melissa smiled, nodded, and subtly pointed out Hillie Clark with one finger. Hillie stood with a cocktail in one hand and a sour, bored look near the bar. She was striking up a conversation with the bartender to bide her time.

Harper and Melissa locked eyes and gave each other a reassuring nod.

Gabriel saw Charlotte coming to get Harper. He silently mouthed "Good luck" to her as Charlotte wrapped an arm around her waist and led her to the middle of the room. Harper's focal piece was hanging on a central pillar. It was enormous in scale, and the vibrant colors varied in depth and shade. The colors swirled together in a bright abstract portrait of *Connie.* Harper created her image highlighted with inflections of white and gold, and her hair looked like white fire.

Charlotte sidled up in front of it, Harper at her side. "Everyone," she began, waving them over. "Gather 'round, your showcase artist this evening has a few words to say about the inspiration for her collection."

Harper was exceptionally nervous as the crowd, murmuring amongst themselves, shuffled over to form a cluster around her. She took strength from their inspiration and took a deep breath. Glancing to her side, she saw Gabriel, her mother, her former arch nemesis, and a small group of women sipping champagne, all looking excited and proud of her. Well, here goes, she thought.

"This piece is yet to be titled because it feels unfinished," she gestured to the portrait. "This work is very special to me. It celebrates an extraordinary friend; one everyone here probably knows. You may have heard about her on the news or from her younger sister, Hillie Clark. Or, maybe she's styled your hair for your prom, your wedding, or even your best friend's wedding. She is one of the kindest, warmest, and smartest people I know, *and* she didn't deserve what happened to her."

Harper paused, took a deep breath, looked out at all the eyes looking back at her, and went on in a slow, serious, deliberate whisper, "but you see, everyone, our Connie, our dear Connie, is *not dead*! She is *not missing!"*

The crowd broke into gasps and hushed whispers, and Harper heard Pearl from the middle thundering, "What on Earth?"

They heard Pearl's horrified grumble and saw Connie's sister, Hillie, looking equally enraged.

Harper forged ahead, knowing she had no choice but to tell all. She took a deep breath, reached into her pocket, pulled out a crumpled, folded paper, and, referring to it, continued.

"When I discovered my friend Connie was missing and encountered the grisly scene myself at her salon, it was all I could do to get to the bottom of what happened. Connie and her salon mean so much to me and everyone who knows her. I wanted her back, to work for her, and mostly, to know what in the world is happening!?"

Harper sighed, "So, I searched and poked around. Er, uh, I mean, *we* searched and poked around," raising her arm and pointing to Melissa." And we found two things.

One, we found a tube of stage adhesive used for applying facial prosthetics; Beauregard sniffed out and found a discarded bag containing buttered scones *and* the tube of stage adhesive," she paused.

"Second, more importantly, while poking about in Connie's office, I saw papers everywhere, but right on top of her desk, there was a paper labeled 'WILL,' so I grabbed it. Connie's will stated, and I quote, '...in *the event of my death, I leave all my belongings, including the salon, to my younger sister, Hillie Clark."* She waved over to Hillie again. *"*Some of you may have met or noticed her resemblance. Hillie, would you like to come on over?"

The crowd craned their collective necks to look over at Hillie; she looked downright furious and refused to budge from her spot by the bar.

Pearl looked equally horrified!

Harper was about to continue when a tall, dark-haired woman in an enormous fur coat stepped out of the crowd. She walked right up to Harper in front of everyone and dead stared at her, then spun around toward the group, whipping the wig off her head.

"*CONNIE*!!!" Everyone gasped!

Connie Clark wasn't dead or missing, after all. She stood in front of the shocked crowd, many faces frozen in disbelief.

Harper took a step forward and kept speaking. "Apparently, many of us took for granted Connie's history in the theater! She learned how to do makeup and, to some extent, some method acting! With some practice and more makeup, Connie masqueraded right before our eyes!"

Harper caught Pearl's eye and noticed her lack of surprise.

The townspeople stared, hanging silently on every word.

"Everyone, please, listen!" Connie apologetically spoke to the crowd, "I have a few apologies. Yes, I faked my death, but with good intentions, I promise. Let me explain. I have been struggling to keep up with business at the salon. I imagined I could fix it so my sister took on my business and set all things financial and such straight. I figured my sister knew more than anyone how much I cared for The Curl Up and Dye. She knew how much I cared for everyone working there. I truly believed you'd all be in good hands." Connie blew her nose while pleading her case.

"I did *not* imagine that my sister would do things *quite* differently, not even close to what I had imagined. I *never* imagined she would do everything she could to sell it—and all my belongings—for her benefit and her benefit alone!" Connie glared at her sister, Hillie, whose eyes darted in every direction as she nervously clutched her hands.

All eyes were on Hillie when Connie turned to Pearl, "And Pearl, I'm so sorry, shug, I should have left the entire salon to *you. You* would have *never* done me wrong, and now, all I've done is include you in this sorry, sad state of sisters and part of a devious mutiny. I thought I was doing something good, but clearly, I didn't know what I was thinking or doing. My head wasn't right. I was desperate, and I am ever so sorry for all this!"

Harper could see tears welling up in Pearl's eyes, and she thought back on all the strange things she could finally connect.

Connie had been around the entire time! The two coffees Pearl brought that morning in the salon were meant for *Connie* and Pearl, not for me. They were secretly going to be meeting, not expecting me to be there.

The special pie that Connie made was her coveted triple chocolate. Pearl had allowed Connie to help from afar and catered the pie to support their friend Charlotte at the gallery opening.

Pearl looked both ashamed and relieved. Keeping her best friend's secret had been weighing on her for weeks. Though she felt relieved, a turbulent wave of guilt hit her.

Connie looked around and found Melissa in the crowd. She stepped through the guests, which parted for her almost out of fear.

Even though having Connie in person was proof Melissa had *not* committed a violent crime, the sordid situation was unsettling, and Melissa had taken the brunt of blame.

Connie used Melissa's monogrammed shears absentmindedly, with no ill will; it had just been bad luck. She faced her now, ashamed and full of remorse.

"I'm so sorry, darlin', so very sorry," she appealed to Melissa. "I never meant to frame *you* for my death. I meant to simply 'pack up and go away' for a while, let my plan play out. While hastily grabbing some of my things in the salon I near cut my hand off with those sharp shears. I bled like a stuck pig and the mess it made allowed for an even more believable scenario. So, I went with it, not thinking things through. I made a mess in there, made it more believable. In my haste, I threw the blasted shears, and they ended up stabbin' my favorite chair. It was reckless and ridiculous and every moment since then I have been a mess trying to figure out how to make it all right. Can you ever forgive me?"

Melissa nodded instantly, marched over to Connie, threw her arms around the woman, and hugged her tightly. There was no doubt, she loved that woman. Connie, relieved, hugged her back.

The crowd gave an 'awww' in unison and regathered in their social cliques chattering away about all the excitement. The event would forever be unforgettable.

THE DAYS FOLLOWING the dramatic art show were chaotic. Connie and Pearl were arrested, it was police procedure, but released after long hours of detailed questioning. They walked off with hefty fines having to make good on the workforce which sprang into action, long hours, and detailed police procedure.

Sorting through the deceit and the damages, Connie spoke with Detectives Boychester and Mumford, who were "madder than two wet hens."

Connie was able to recoup and recover control of her salon with the help of her supportive neighbors and friends. She also recovered her belongings, which Hillie had prepped and planned to sell in an estate sale. Connie did not press charges but made it clear to Hillie that she was not welcome in her world and wished her well in having to live with herself. Connie figured that was punishment enough.

FINALLY GATHERED TOGETHER at The Curl Up and Dye, the gals settled right into sharing and giggling with one another. Comforted among her favorite people, Harper shared with the gang how the art exhibit guests actually believed the drama was *part of her art show!*

"Can you believe guests would think we made a scene as a form of 'live art!' Well, I guess good entertainment sure helps with sales! I did amazing! I even stashed away enough to secure my partnership for several months! Connie, who would have thought your antics would ultimately be for the good and help with seed money for my boutique space?"

"Well, shug, it was never my intention to take the long road to that end, but I guess if we want to turn my meltdown into something positive, by all means, I'm all for it. You are such a dear to me, and your loyal friendship is humbling for me; I don't think I deserve you. I never would have been able to cover the legal fines for Pearl and myself. However it came together, I'm happy and ever so grateful for your generosity in taking care of it all. My dear, you have dibs on all the triple chocolate pie I can make for you forever! My treat, of course! "

The salon girls knew Harper had used funds from selling several pieces of art to help pay off Connie's crushing debt, the entire reason she had faked her death in the first place. The gals felt a renewed sense of friendship and a loving bond.

"I have one other condition, Connie," Harper added for all to hear.

Connie, who stood behind Harper with a comb mid-way through her hair, stopped. "Anything, shug…what'll it be?"

A mischievous smile slipped over Harper's face as she said very deliberately, "You make Melissa *and* me hairstylists here at The Curl, officially!"

Melissa sat a few feet away, her feet in a bubbling mini-spa tub, reclining with cucumber slices. Hearing Harper, she sat up quickly, cucumber slices falling off her face, she was riveted, awaiting Connie's response.

Connie lowered her comb and looked thoughtfully over to Melissa, then back to Harper, who was twisting around in her chair to gaze up at Connie, grinning with wide-eyed expectation.

After anxious silence, Connie set down her comb deliberately and walked into the back room. She returned with two aprons and a massive smile on her face. She tossed an apron to Melissa, and she tossed an apron to Harper. The girls looked at one another in mutual admiration and glee.

Connie took a deep breath as the girls held up their salon aprons with all the bedazzled "C's" on them. Inhaling the aromas of her beloved salon, freshly brewed coffee mixed with fumes of hairspray and nail polish, she placed her hands on her hips and delivered her announcement to the room:

"Ya'll start tomorrow, ladies; welcome to the *Curl Up and Dye!*"

THANK you for reading my book, Shear Fear at The Curl Up and Dye!

If you loved this book, I think you will enjoy the first book in my new series:

Dastardly Deceit and The Bow Wow Bakery
A Doggy Bakery Cozy Mystery Series
PET OWNERS ARE THRILLED with their small town's new doggy bakery until murder threatens their freshly baked treats!

After moving from New York City back to her hometown of Glenwood Falls, Sophie Harrington wants a quiet life with her sweet sable weenie dog Max.

She opens Max's Bow Wow Bakery, a shop for furry friends who visit excitedly and wag their tails while munching on delicious baked treats.

Sophie's friend, Hadley, owns the Needlework Trading Post next door, specializing in knit doggy vests and sweaters—the two team up to prepare their booths for anticipated festival profits.

Excitement suddenly stops when Sophie discovers a dead body next door to the bakery! Colton Worthington, a fierce local CEO, is dead, and it's clear his death was not an accident.

Sophie realizes it's up to her, Hadley, Max, and a handsome friend from the past to find out who's responsible before the jeopardized Fall Festival is canceled for good.

*** *Doggy Treat recipes included!* ***

Continue reading Dastardly Deceit and The Bow Wow Bakery

LET'S *keep reading great cozies!*

To be sure and catch the next novel by Belinda Page, sign up for the newsletter:

Belinda's Cozy Clan Newsletter - Join!

FOLLOW BELINDA'S AUTHOR PAGES:

AMAZON BELINDA'S Page

GOODREADS BELINDA'S Page

BOOKBUB BELINDA'S Page

BOOKSPROUT BELINDA'S Page

SEE YOU IN THE PAGES!
  Belinda

Made in the USA
Coppell, TX
22 November 2024